RAVENKIN

VIOLA TEMPEST

CONTENTS

RAVENKIN

VIOLA TEMPEST

A LOW, ANGRY HOWL ECHOED UP THE STAIRS, AND Elise knew she was late. Again.

Mrs. Gallagher threw open her bedroom door, the wood slamming against the drywall with a sharp *thud*! Elise squinted as the sunlight streamed in through the window. She eyed the wall and found the dent from the door handle a full-fledged hole in the drywall now.

"Elise Marie Winters—get up!" Mrs. Gallagher shrieked. "This is the third time this week that you've ignored your alarm and missed the bus!"

Elise waved a hand at her, trying to mentally quiet the woman's ringing voice. She sat up in bed.

"I know. I'm sorry, okay? I'm going."

Mrs. Gallagher slapped her hand down and threw off her blankets. "Get up. Right this instant!"

Elise grumbled as she pushed herself into a standing position. Her head swirled, and her vision blotted at the corners at the sudden movement, but she didn't dare sit back down in front of the headmaster. Mrs. Gallagher thrusted the clothes, folded neatly, atop Elise's dresser and into her arms.

"Get dressed, and be downstairs in two minutes. If I have to come up here one more time, so help me—"

Elise flinched as the door slammed shut again behind the woman. She stuck her tongue out at the trembling wood and pulled on her clothes. She then threw her knotted hair into a high, messy bun and pushed her few bracelets, mismatched and handmade by the younger kids in her orphanage, up past her wrists. And finally, she tugged on her black boots and jogged down the steps to the first floor.

"Finally!" Mrs. Gallagher called out when she caught sight of her. She threw Elise's backpack into her arms, and Elise flinched as the corner of her textbook inside stabbed at her chest. "And you didn't even clean up your mess from last night, either. How fitting."

The woman shoved the notebooks, paperwork, and homework that Elise had been working on into her arms. Papers crumpled, her notebooks dropped to the floor, and her notes scattered around her in a fluttering pile. Her blood heated, simmering just under the surface.

Elise set her backpack onto the floor so she could organize her papers neatly into her binders. But Mrs. Gallagher's harsh voice echoed in the vaulted main room.

"You've managed to make us all late, you've missed your bus, you've left a mess here, *and* after all that, you can't even pick up your pace when you need to rush a little? Honestly, Elise—can't you make anything easy?" She huffed, sipping at her Starbucks cup as the ring on her finger glimmered in the sun's rays shining in.

Elise gritted her teeth. "I forgot to set my alarm. I already said sorry."

"And you'll say it again and again day after day because you can't seem to do anything right."

Her words bit deep, chewing out a chunk of Elise's heart and spitting it onto the floor. She knew she wasn't perfect, she knew it was a privilege to be given a room and housing at her orphanage, especially in her older, teenage years. She knew that.

And yet, Mrs. Gallagher seemed to enjoy pushing her to her limits. She basked in the power and control that running the orphanage had given her. And if insulting, overworking, and abusing children wasn't bad enough, she also kept most of the funds she got from tax exemptions and government assistance, and used it toward her own lavish life-style. Elise eyed the coffee cup, a ring of red lipstick around its rim.

She reeled in the anger bubbling under her skin.

"Once you finish, you need to go." Mrs. Gallagher spat before eyeing her long, painted nails.

Elise slid her backpack over her shoulders and moved toward the kitchen, but Mrs. Gallagher grabbed her arm and yanked her toward the front door.

"You're late enough, child. Let's go."

"Wait! My lunch—!" Elise called, eyeing the brown paper bag on the counter, jutting out from the window to the kitchen.

"Too late. You made us wait, so you'll have to wait to eat until tonight." Mrs. Gallagher eyed her. Elise looked back in cold, angry confusion, but Mrs. Gallagher smirked. "Fair is only fair, right?"

She dragged Elise to the front door and stopped just inside its threshold. And when her grip loosened a fraction of an inch, Elise yanked her arm away.

"Get going," Mrs. Gallagher said flatly.

Elise glanced out the door. "I need a ride."

Mrs. Gallagher snorted. "No, Elise. You've lost that privilege. You can walk."

"But—!"

"I don't want to hear it!"

"I could just ride in the van with the younger kids!

The elementary school is right next door to the high school. You could drop me off!"

Mrs. Gallagher propped a hand on her hip, and that disgusting duck-lipped pout of hers overtook her face.

"Again—you've lost that privilege today, sweetie. Now, I suggest you start running before the bell rings at school, and you're late again. You remember what happened last time you were late, don't you?"

Elise swallowed past the lump in her throat. How could she forget? She had knelt on salt for thirty minutes straight, and had the bruises from it on her knees for a week.

Mrs. Gallagher shoved her through the door, and Elise cringed as the thick wood slammed shut behind her. She turned and glared at the poster hanging on its front.

Fleming's Orphanage: The Beginning to Family and Lifelong Love.

Elise spat on the models' smiling faces. It was a lie. It was all a lie. It had always been a lie. And no one knew—no one cared.

Elise let out a slow breath, trying to regain her composure, and that was when the door creaked open behind her. She glanced over her shoulder and found the youngest caretaker, Ms. Augustine, smiling in the crack of the doorway. She held out Elise's bagged lunch.

"Here, take it," she whispered.

Elise grabbed the bag and stuffed it into her back-pack. She gave Ms. Augustine a warm smile, the heat in her blood dissipating slightly.

"Thanks."

Ms. Augustine nodded quickly. "You have a great day at school, okay? And good luck on your math test. I know you'll do great."

Elise smiled at her, all traces of her anger fading as a pool of new anxiety took over. She had spent the last three nights preparing for her math test. Ms. Augustine had stayed up late with her each night to make sure she understood the problems inside and out. Elise could never thank her enough for all she had done and continued to do. But at the very least, she could prove to her caretaker her worth. She could show Ms. Augustine that all her hard work and kindness weren't for nothing. Elise wouldn't just survive—she would thrive.

Mrs. Gallagher's furious howl echoed from inside, and Ms. Augustine winced. She waved goodbye to Elise and gave her one more cheer of support before clicking the door shut behind her.

Elise shrugged on her backpack again and took a steadying breath before racing toward her school. She ran ten blocks, through three acres of property, up two flights of stairs, and crashed into her seat, just as the final bell chimed its warning. She leaned back in her chair and desperately tried to catch her breath. Needles prickled her lungs, and a cramp in her side made her grimace, but hey, at least Mrs. Gallagher couldn't say she was late.

She pulled her books out from her bag and laid them gently on the desk for her first class—English. She paid special attention to her textbook for the class as its cover was torn, and its spine was withering with age.

The pages of the book barely stayed glued in place; she'd probably have to tape the thing soon. Everyone else around her pulled out new textbooks with shiny covers and perfectly intact pages. Elise couldn't help but feel more than a little ashamed of her own copy. But it was all she could afford; well—it was all Mrs. Gallagher was willing to buy for her.

The headmaster found it ridiculous and a waste of money to buy books at all for Elise's public-school classes. Which she wouldn't have to do normally, but Elise was in the advanced English class. Something one would think Mrs. Gallagher would be proud of and eager to support, but her rolled eyes and skimpy dollars given for Elise's cost of materials proved otherwise.

"Alright, everyone. Let me finish writing the notes on the board, and we can begin," Mr. Lincomb said, his back turned to the class as he scribbled away on the board.

Everyone around her mumbled and whispered to each other as they settled in, but Elise sat quietly on her own. She had friends of her own. Beth was her closest friend and confidant, and Elise got to enjoy living with her and sharing a room at the orphanage. But she was three years behind her and didn't share any classes with Elise.

Other than Beth… well, her friends consisted of seven-year-old Lily and eleven-year-old Thomas, her other two roommates at the orphanage. They were sweet and loving, and she couldn't imagine living at a place like that without them there. The two were like siblings of her own, and she tried her very best to make sure they were protected from Mrs. Gallagher's anger. They were, truthfully, the only family she really had.

Elise couldn't remember her parents. She was told that they were taken from her in a bad car accident when she was only two years old. They were young, barely out of high school when they had her.

Elise liked to imagine they were desperately, irrevocably in love with each other. When they discovered that her mother was pregnant with Elise, they were overjoyed. And when they held her as a newborn, they cradled her with love and warmth. She imagined they loved her—she hoped they loved her. But they were young, immature, and underprepared for the worst. So, when the car crashed and both of them were killed, Elise was left alone in the world without any documentation as to what should happen to her.

Without a will to defer to, nor any extended family that could be reached, Elise was turned over to the adoption system and placed in Fleming's Orphanage.

Which was where she had been ever since, much to Mrs. Gallagher's annoyance. But the woman wouldn't have to deal with her much longer; she was to turn eighteen in just one more year, and then she'd age out of the system. Gone forever from her one and only home, from her only family, from all her friends... she didn't like to think about that day.

Elise was thrown out of her thoughts when something wet shot at the back of her neck. She gritted her teeth, knowing exactly who and what shot the spitball at her. She clenched a fist, but refrained from turning around. They weren't worth it, she reminded herself. They were dumb and immature, and they only wanted to get a rise from her. She could—

Another spitball flew and slid down the back of her shirt. She whipped around and scowled at Owen, Jack, and Tyler, snickering in their seats. Jack didn't even try to hide the straw in his hand.

"Really? Spitballs? How old are you, five?" Elise snapped.

Jack shot another one right at her face. Elise slapped it away.

"You seem extra mad today, Elise. Are you on your period?" Owen taunted. Tyler and Jack chuckled.

Elise glared at him. "You're immature and disgusting. Stop spitting stuff at me."

"What are you gonna do about it? Tell on us?" Tyler teased.

The last time she tried to get a teacher's support

after the relentless bullying that Owen and the others had graced her with, *she* ended up being called the "troublemaker" and labeled as "wanting attention." And the icing on the top was the detention slip she received that day.

Her fist tightened on her lap.

Before Elise could snap back, her textbook was yanked from her desk. She grabbed for it, but she was too slow. Raquel, seated at the desk beside her, dangled the book in the air.

"Ew, look at this thing. Couldn't your parents buy you a better copy? Oh, wait—you have none." She hawked out a laugh, and the boys behind her mirrored her.

"Give it back," Elise murmured tightly.

"No, I don't think I will." Raquel threw the book over to her right, to the next seat where the Queen Bee herself sat.

Brittney laughed at the shoddy book as she spun it around in her hands. "You know, I think this book is perfect for Elise. A sad, rundown book for a sad, little orphan girl like her. It's exactly what she deserves."

The others snickered, and Brittney gave her that pointed gaze. Elise's fingers clenched so hard on her lap, her knuckles blacked white.

"Give it back," she repeated. But the blonde bitch opened the cover instead.

Brittney flipped through the loose pages and chuckled aloud. "How is this thing still together? It's falling apart. I wouldn't be surprised if the pages just —" she tore a handful of pages from the spine, "fell out."

"Stop!" Elise cried out.

"Quiet down, Elise." Mr. Lincomb said from the front of the room. Brittney threw the book to Raquel, who slid it back onto Elise's desk just before he turned around. "Alright, class, let's begin."

Raquel held out the torn pages for Elise. She went to grab them, but the girl dropped them before she could. They fluttered to the floor around her feet to a cacophony of snickers all around her. Elise held back burning tears as she grabbed the pages on the floor and started taping them back into place.

CHAPTER

TWO

Elise failed her math test that day. And got detention—again.

In math class, she tried her very best to focus on the test before her and remember all of the equations and formulas she had studied with Ms. Augustine over the course of the last three days. But no matter how much the test, she couldn't even begin to give it her best because of the others around her.

Jack tapped his foot over and over and over again beside her. Owen threw bits of paper at her back. And Brittney took her eraser so she had to write, scribble out her mistakes, and write again—over and over. By the time the clock was up, Elise hurried to write something —anything in the blank spots on her paper.

But her teacher called for pencils to be put down. She collected the tests and handed them back at the end of class. She gave Elise her copy with a disappointed shake of her head. Elise tried to tell her she couldn't concentrate. She tried to tell her that she didn't have the right supplies when her teacher criticized her scribbling everything out instead of erasing. She tried to explain herself, but the teacher wanted none of it.

Elise finally busted.

"They're sabotaging me!" she cried out in front of everyone. The whole classroom went silent.

"What are you talking about, Elise?"

"I'm talking about them—Owen, Jack, Brittney— they actively sabotaged me so I couldn't focus, and I'd do badly."

The teacher sighed. "Elise, it's not okay for you to blame others for your lack of preparation today."

"I did prepare!" she cried. "I studied for three whole days and practiced my problems for hours with Ms. Augustine. I tried to prepare as best I could, and yet *these people* wouldn't stop bothering me long enough to let me take my test."

Everyone around her watched with wide eyes as Elise shook with uncontained anger. She couldn't do this anymore. She couldn't put up with this abuse both at the orphanage and at school; it wasn't fair. Surely, her teacher would see she wasn't in the wrong. Surely, she knew Elise and her history of good grades and knew Elise wouldn't just fail a math test completely. Surely, she would see it—right?

The teacher eyed the others. "Jack, Owen, Brittney —is she telling the truth?"

The three of them looked at each other before the puppy dog eyes came out.

"We were just taking our tests, too. I would never intentionally try to sabotage someone. That would be cruel," Brittney stated, making her voice higher and softer to work with her honey sweet words.

"Yeah. We were just minding our own business," Owen said.

"I can barely pass math as it is. I'm not gonna waste time 'sabotaging' someone else during a test," Jack said easily.

Elise gazed at the teacher. Surely, she wouldn't believe them. Their shit-eating grins were so obvious, so fake, so forced—

"Alright, Elise. Now, you can't blame others for your problems. If you were underprepared and stressed out, that's one thing. But you cannot blame the others for that. Do you understand?"

"But I'm telling you—I *was* prepared! They—" Elise started, but the teacher cut her short.

"That's enough. You need to take responsibility for your actions. I won't have senseless blame and finger-pointing in my classroom."

" But—!"

"*Enough*, Elise."

Elise sat silently, the objections pushing and shoving to get past her lips. The teacher grabbed a yellow slip of paper and scribbled on it on her desk. Elise knew what was coming before that yellow slip even landed on her desk.

"I will see you after school today in detention. Don't be late."

The others snickered at her as the teacher concluded class and dismissed them all. Elise shoved her test into her backpack without organizing it nicely in her binder like she did for everything else. She rushed out of the room, feeling twenty sets of eyes on her back as the hallway outside filled up.

She finished out the rest of her day in silence and turned up at detention, only to find her teacher waiting with a frown. She asked Elise if her opinions had changed from earlier after she had some time to reflect. Elise told her no with a huff. She wasn't the one who was wrong here, nor would she pretend to be.

The teacher made her write on the old chalkboard for an hour and a half straight, *I will not lie. I will take responsibility for my actions.* As Elise marched out of the school building and headed toward the park near the orphanage, she couldn't get the squeaky sound of the chalk scraping across the board out of her mind.

She bundled up against the chill creeping in behind the last dim rays of sunlight for the day. Fall was finally beginning to transform into winter, and by the chill settling in her bones, Elise could tell. She nestled deeper into her hoodie.

She walked on for more than twenty minutes until she reached the bend in the sidewalk that led up to the park—*her* park. Well, it wasn't exactly hers, but she liked to think it was because of her daily attendance.

She plopped down on the first bench off to the right among the trees. Most people didn't use this bench because of its seclusion and offset from the main path. But that's exactly why Elise liked it. She dropped her backpack on the metal beside her and looked up, but they weren't there. The ravens.

There was a flock of them that always kept her company there. She would pull out the bread crusts or snacks she kept from her school lunch and leave them to the ravaging birds. She'd always watch as they dug in, pecking and squawking with delight at her gifts. She laughed at their joy and enjoyed sitting close enough to study them.

There were five of them total, and each had markings or traits that set them apart from the others. Her favorite, however, was the one with the clipped beak. It was always gentle with her and moved slowly and purposefully.

Elise glanced around the nearby path and up in the trees, but she caught no sight of the majestic birds. She sighed as she leaned back on the cool metal bars and closed her eyes. Maybe they had flown off, tired of waiting after her tardiness. She didn't blame them.

She let the darkness her eyelids provided her envelope her. She let out a long, heavy breath, feeling the tension in her shoulders and neck. The crumpled-up math test burned her like a brand, sitting, waiting, judging from inside her bag.

With its memory, came back moments of her terrible day. Nothing had gone right from the beginning—*nothing*. Would anything ever go right for her? She had nothing of her own, nothing to call hers. All she owned was her future, and even then, as she tried desperately to advance in school and work her hardest to get good grades so she could set up a solid plan for success—she was beaten down and labeled a liar.

She stared into the darkness and called out to whoever or whatever might be listening. Why did fate give her this life? Had she done something wrong before? Was it a cruel joke? Or were the others right? Did she actually, really... deserve this?

A fluttering sound in front of her pulled her from the darkness. She opened her eyes to find a raven perched on the stone wall opposite the bench. She looked at its beak and found the tip of the top half chipped. She smiled.

"Hello, my friend. I'm sorry I'm late today. I got caught up in detention at school. But don't worry, I have your snacks."

She dug around in her bag for the plastic baggie of bread crusts she had saved. Once she found them, she ripped open the bag and held up a piece before finding the other four ravens gathered on each side of the first one. She greeted them, too, and tossed the bread-crumbs to them, one for each. The birds picked at their snacks, and she smiled as she watched them.

So big and dark and beautiful. Their wings flapped wide occasionally, and Elise was always surprised to see how wide their wingspan actually was. Their feathers shimmered in the waning light, and their little eyes reflected light like orbs. Something in her chest clenched and twisted with ache. She wished she could be free and wild like these birds. They were dark and mysterious like shadows, but also sweet and gentle and loyal as they came to visit her every day. She gave them snacks and conversation, and in turn, they gave her company, and occasionally, lost things.

She kept a box under her bed at the orphanage

with a collection of those lost things. Coins, scraps of fabric and aluminum, buttons, shiny pieces of glass... Elise cherished her collection. No one, not even her friends, was allowed to touch that box.

Elise glanced up when a woman pacing down the path made her way toward the bench. She huffed as she pushed a gigantic stroller. Only one child sat inside while the other danced and skipped around her, laughing at her struggling. As she approached the bench, the birds stopped their pecking and perched silently on the stone wall. She eyed them before waving a hand.

"Shoo!" she called out, wings flapping and fluttering as the birds flew up into the nearest tree.

Before she could stop herself, Elise crossed her arms. "Why did you do that? They weren't bothering anyone."

The woman eyed Elise as if just noticing her presence for the first time. "They're just dumb birds." She huffed.

Elise leaned forward, that heat in her blood coming to a simmer yet again.

"They aren't dumb. Ravens are one of the smartest birds in existence. And besides, they're not doing anything wrong. They're existing and doing the best they can to survive, just like all of us."

The woman snorted as she pushed the stroller around the bench and made her way back up the pathway. "They're ravens, dear. They're creepy, little thieves. They don't do anything or help anyone, so what's the point?"

Elise stared at the woman as she retreated with the stroller and her other child in hand. Slowly, the birds fluttered back down to the ground and resumed munching on their sandwich bits. Elise clenched and unclenched her fist again and again. What was wrong with people? How could they be so heartless?

"I'm sorry about that. That lady doesn't know anything. I think you guys are... sweet." She smiled at them. "You're my friends, and no matter what anyone else says, you all deserve to live, thrive, and be happy, just like everybody else."

One of the birds, the one with the chipped beak, hopped down from the stone wall and stopped at her feet. It dropped something on the ground before her, and then turned and flew off with the rest of them. Elise bent down and grabbed the coin on the ground, but found it not to be a regular coin, but an arcade token. She smiled as she pocketed the gift.

She then closed her backpack and slid it back onto her shoulders before making her back to the orphanage.

Mrs. Gallagher greeted her with more yelling, more cursing, and more threats than before. Her math teacher called her, apparently, who enlight-

ened her about Elise's failed math test and her arguing
during class, which led to her detention. Elise let the
woman scream and yell at her, finding it better to just
deal with it than try to fight back at this point. She
turned the token over and over between her fingers as
she faced the wrath of the headmaster.

Eventually, Elise made it up to her room, and
there, Lily, Thomas, and Beth waited for her on their
bunks.

"How did it go?" Thomas gave her an empathetic
look.

Elise shrugged before dropping onto her bed.
"About as well as usual. She hates me."

Beth looked at her from the bottom bunk opposite
her. "To be fair, she hates everyone."

"Yeah, but especially me." Elise sighed before
another thought flickered to life in her mind. "Lily!
You had your meeting today. How'd that go?"

Little Lily, small and careful and fragile, ducked
her head from her spot on Beth's mattress.

"Mr. and Mrs. Fermin were very nice. They were
so nice! And they loved my polka dot dress, and they
said I looked like a perfect fit for their family. They
were excited to meet me at first." Lily mumbled the last
part.

Beth squeezed her hand.

"Then what happened?" Elise asked.

Beth gave Elise a dark look. "Mrs. Gallagher
happened, that's what."

"Mrs. Gallagher told them about my sickness all the time. I tried to tell them it wasn't anything serious, and it was mostly just colds and allergies and stuff. But she wouldn't stop talking about how much money she had to spend to make me better again."

"Oh, Lily." Elise's expression softened.

Lily sniffled, wiping at her eyes with tiny fists. Beth held her close to her side.

"She didn't even let me tell them myself! I could have shown them I was worth it. They could have brought me home with them. But—but—"

Lily broke out in tears, and Beth pulled her into a tight hug. Thomas watched silently from the bunk above Elise, but she could feel the tension in the room like a blanket. Elise fumed on her bunk as Lily sobbed. Lily—who was the gentlest, kindest, sweetest person she knew.

Lily should've been adopted ages ago, and she had many opportunities to be, but Mrs. Gallagher always foiled those meetings. Beth and Elise figured she did so in order to keep all the kids here longer. Then she wouldn't have to take on many new ones due to the lack of space.

She could retain control and power over them, and she wouldn't lose potential government funding for her efforts here. It seemed obvious to her—if the kids didn't get adopted, she'd keep receiving more money to care for them. Money that was, instead, going right into her own wallet.

Once Lily's sniffles died down, Elise took a steadying breath so as not to overload the tiny girl with her raging thoughts.

"It'll happen, Lil. One day, the right couple will come along and sweep you out of here. Today just wasn't that day," Elise said softly.

Lily sniffled. "But how? No one's going to want me when Mrs. Gallagher always makes a big deal of my illnesses."

"One day, a couple is going to come in here, and no matter how Mrs. Gallagher treats you, and no matter what she throws out about your health issues, this couple isn't going to care. Because once they see how sweet and kind and caring you are, they're going to love you, no matter what. Okay?"

Lily stared at her with red-rimmed eyes. Elise reached out and squeezed her knee.

"Okay?" she repeated.

Lily nodded slowly. "Okay."

"Good. Now go to bed. It's time to sleep, and I'm sure you're tired after a long day."

Elise helped Lily onto her top bunk and tucked her in once she was settled. She nestled Lily's stuffed bunny into the crook of her arm, and Lily squeezed it tight. Elise gave her a final kiss on her forehead and smiled at her friend. Lily managed the smallest of smiles herself, and Elise hoped that by the morning, her smile would replace her sniffles.

Beth slid under her covers, and Thomas rolled

onto his stomach. Elise flipped out the lights and moved to get onto her own bed, but she stopped when the door cracked open and in peeked Ms. Augustine. She smiled at Elise and waved her into the hall. Elise followed, and the two of them sat on the carpet in the hallway, leaning against the wall outside the bedroom.

"How'd your math test go today?" Ms. Augustine asked with hopeful eyes and smile lines.

Elise shook her head as she stared at her lap, unable to meet her eyes. "I failed."

Ms. Augustine was quiet for a moment. "But we studied so hard, and you seemed to have a handle on it. What happened?"

"It doesn't matter. None of it matters," she murmured.

"Elise, what's going on? Tell me so I can help you."

Elise shrugged helplessly. "You can't help me. No one can. My classmates hate me and pick on me relentlessly, my teachers ignore the bullying and make it my fault somehow, all my school supplies are old and barely held together, Mrs. Gallagher doesn't care about me or my future and just wants me out of here while sabotaging everyone else's meetings, and I—I can't do *anything* to fix any of it!"

Ms. Augustine sat with her in silence, letting Elise catch her breath and giving her the chance to cool down before her gentle, soothing voice murmured.

"Elise, you know you're not alone, right? You're

never alone. And you have a support system in place to help you through these hard times—"

"What support system? You? Lily? Thomas? Beth? They're all kids, and you—you're powerless against Mrs. Gallagher. So, don't tell me I have a support system if the system in place is failing."

"Elise—"

"Things would just be better if I were gone. No Mrs. Gallagher, no school, no classmates, no stuffy adopters—I'd be free of it all."

"Elise, you can't think that way. Lily, Thomas, Beth —they all love you. They need you as much as I and the rest of us do. You aren't alone, and you are so, so loved."

Elise glanced at her and found Ms. Augustine's expression sad and grim. Something in her chest twisted with regret at her words, but she didn't care to take them back. She pushed herself up.

"I'm going to bed. I'm tired."

"Okay," Ms. Augustine stood up, too. "Will you be okay?" she whispered as Elise stopped in her open doorway.

To most people, the idea of a new day meant a fresh start. She could do things better. She could wake up on time for school. She could catch the bus and avoid Mrs. Gallagher's wrath. She could ignore the others at school and focus on her classes. She could get on the teachers' good side and get their support if the others wouldn't give up. She could pass her tests. She could come back at the end of the night to no yelling, no punishments, and talk with her friends happily in their room. But Elise didn't believe in any of that. Tomorrow was nothing more than a chance to repeat today, and chances were, it would be.

Elise glanced over her shoulder at the caretaker. "I'll be fine."

With that, she shut the door behind her and flopped onto her bed in the darkness. Soft, rhythmic breaths surrounded her, and she let herself relax. She pulled the arcade token from her pocket and ran her thumb over its smooth surface again and again until she dozed off into a dark so similar to the shade of a raven's wing.

After yet another frustrating and long day at school, Elise celebrated the end of the week and woke up excited for the weekend. She finished her homework the night before so she wouldn't have to worry about any of it while she was off. Then she shoved and rushed her way through the weekend chores that Mrs. Gallagher assigned to all the children.

Elise swept the main room, cleaned the kitchen,

from head to toe, polished the bathroom that many of them shared on the upper floor, and dusted and tidied up her shared bedroom. The bedroom was supposed to be worked on as a team with whoever the orphans shared it with, but because of Elise, they kept their bedroom fairly tidy all the time, so it required minimal cleaning on the weekends—just as Elise liked.

Once she finished her list, Elise headed toward the headmaster's office to tell Mrs. Gallagher that she was through with her chores. Mrs. Gallagher made it a requirement for everyone to notify her when they finished so she could inspect their work. If she gave the go-ahead, the children were free to do whatever they wanted for the rest of the day. But if she thought things needed more work, then they were stuck doing even more cleaning.

Elise made sure Mrs. Gallagher would have nothing to complain about when it came to her chores.

She knocked on the closed door and heard Mrs. Gallagher call her in from inside. Elise propped open the door and peeked her head inside.

"I'm finished with my chores Mrs.—" Elise's voice fizzled out as she caught sight of the couple sitting on the chairs before Mrs. Gallagher's desk.

They turned to look at her and smiled kindly. The man had peppered hair, slicked back from his slightly receding hairline. He had a mole under his right eye and deep wrinkles on his forehead, but he didn't look too old in appearance.

The woman was younger but had graying hairs sprouting from her temples. She dressed in a knee-length dress, belted at the waist, with patterned stockings poking out from underneath. She reminded Elise of the art teacher at her school.

"Oh, Elise. How perfect. Come in, and have a seat. I was just about to come out and retrieve you." Mrs. Gallagher smiled, her voice sickly sweet.

Elise closed the door behind her and sat at the edge of the third chair seated to the side of the desk. All three adults smiled at her, but Elise couldn't smile back. Something was... off-kilter in this room.

"Elise, this is Mr. and Mrs. Gregor. They are interested in adopting a child here and have requested to meet the oldest child we have. Which, incidentally, is you."

Elise stared at Mrs. Gallagher as her words processed in her mind. These people... wanted to meet her? Nobody ever wanted to meet her. She was seventeen, and the oldest at the orphanage. Once an orphan got past thirteen, fourteen years old, people didn't want them anymore. They were too old, practically a young adult. And when people chose to adopt, they usually want a fresh start, not a preteen with behavioral problems and a world of memories under their belt.

"Elise? Say something, dear."

Elise almost flinched at her pet name. Never *once* had Mrs. Gallagher called her "dear." It felt... wrong. She preferred her insults and curses instead.

"Why?" Elise mumbled.

Mr. Gregor cleared his throat. "My wife and I have done many, many hours of research on the childcare and adoption system, and how it works. We learned that once kids hit a certain age, they are less likely to get adopted, and chances are, they age out of the system. So, we decided to go a different direction and adopt a child who's older and is statistically less likely to get chosen."

"Plus, we don't want a baby or a small child. As I'm sure you can tell, we are a bit older than many other adopters are." Mrs. Gregor chuckled. "We want a child we can call our own and make a part of our family, but one who has a life, memories, and opinions of their own already. We're excited about that."

Mrs. Gregor smiled at Elise, and she awkwardly smiled back. Was this really happening? Were these people really interested... in her?

"Splendid! A sweet sentiment, really." Mrs. Gallagher gave them one of her nicest fake smiles.

"Yes, so if you don't mind. Elise, can we ask you a few questions?" Mrs. Gregor directed at her.

Elise shrugged. "Sure."

"Great! Okay, first things first, we heard you are seventeen years old and a senior in high school this year. How is that going?"

Elise's eyes wavered to Mrs. Gallagher. While her smile stayed intact, the woman's eyes bulged as if to warn her. Elise took a steadying breath.

"It's, um, going well so far."

"What is your favorite subject in school?"

"Biology and history."

"Interesting combination. Why those two?"

Elise shrugged again. "I enjoy learning about animals and their habits. And history is fun to learn about. It seems all stuffy at first, but then you realize how goofy people were, and that they were people just like you and I, and then it's funny."

Mrs. Gregor chuckled. "That is true. And very insightful."

"Yes, Elise has always had a very... interesting mind," Mrs. Gallagher threw in.

Elise's gaze hardened on her, but the Gregor's looked up in question.

"What do you mean?" Mrs. Gregor asked.

"Well, while she has had decent grades in school, she frequently gets in trouble for behavioral issues, talking back to teachers, picking fights with her classmates, and tardiness. It's a shame, really. She's so smart, and yet she doesn't recognize or act on her full potential. We are working on that, of course, but it will take time and much guidance."

Elise's nostrils flared. Wait—*wait*—!

"Oh, that's... unfortunate," Mr. Gregor said, his voice lowering.

"Yes, indeed. And not to mention her lack of friends her own age, and even her oddities."

"Oddities?" Mrs. Gregor raised a brow. "What do you mean?"

"Well, my daughter just so happens to be the same age as Elise and a classmate of hers. And she's told me all about Elise's after-school trips to the park where she—oh goodness, it's more difficult than I thought to say out loud." The Gregor couple watched and waited in eager silence.

Elise held her breath. No—no, no, no—

"Brittney has said she's witnessed Elise talking to crows in the park. But not just once or twice—every single day."

The Gregors looked at her in question, and Elise could only stare at Mrs. Gallagher. Brittney—Brittney Gallagher followed her after school. She *followed* her to the park, and she saw her interact with the ravens. She told her mother about it, and Mrs. Gallagher wanted to use this information to bomb her first meeting in *seven—years—*

"That is a bit... odd." Mrs. Gregor relinquished.

Elise clenched her fingers into white knuckled fists on her lap. She shook in her seat.

"They're ravens," she mumbled through tight lips.

Mrs. Gallagher raised a brow at her. "Oh, even better. Dirty, thieving ravens."

"They *aren't* thieving. They are kind and gentle, and they are loyal to me," Elise snapped, her control slipping.

Mrs. Gallagher sensed this, and Elise could make out the hint of a smirk on her painted pink lips.

"They are wild birds, dear. They're loyal to no one but their stomachs."

"They're not! They're my friends!" Elise's voice rose dangerously.

Mrs. Gallagher knew it then, and she struck the final blow.

"Oh, I guess you finally made some friends after all. Too bad they're not human."

Elise bolted up from her chair, her finger waving angrily through the air as her cheeks burned. "You know absolutely *nothing* about me or my friendships or my life. Those 'dirty, thieving ravens' have treated me with more respect and care than you ever have in the fourteen years I've lived here!"

Mrs. Gallagher chuckled humorlessly and waved at her. "Dear, settle down. We're in a meeting with your potential adopters! Dear, me. I'm so very sorry for her outburst." She turned her poisoned honey voice to the couple, who watched the outburst with wide eyes. "Clearly, this one needs more guidance than I thought."

"*Guidance!* When have you ever offered me guidance? You much prefer insulting me, criticizing me, abusing me, and making me feel worthless more than you offer any kind of *guidance*. You know—I'm sick of you. I'm sick of this place. I'm sick of this stupid system and it's stupid orphanages and it's stupid employees like you who take advantage of it."

"Now, now." Mrs. Gallagher tried to quiet her, but Elise was having none of it.

"You treat me like garbage, and then you expect me to look up to you. You mistreat me, and then expect me to respect you. You manipulate and hurt me, and then wonder why I get so upset. Don't you see it?" Elise turned to the couple, her hands held up in wide saucers. "Don't *you*?"

Mrs. Gregor leaned into her husband, getting as far as possible from Elise. He touched her arm in reassurance. Both of them looked at her with wide eyes, and that's when Elise realized her mistake. Mrs. Gallagher had won again. She riled her up, forced her to crack, and then ruined her last probable chance at adoption. And she fell for it.

She blew it for herself.

Mrs. Gallagher cleared her throat. "Mr. and Mrs. Gregor, I am so sorry for that display. Truthfully, I thought Elise might be a good match for you. But clearly, we have some more to work on. I apologize."

The older couple nodded, shifting awkwardly in their seats.

No—she thought, *no, no, please, give me another chance.*

"Now, I know you're looking for a slightly older child. While Elise is the oldest we have, there are many others who are only a few years behind her. Why don't we have a look at their bios, and I can point you in a better direction."

The couple nodded, and Mrs., Gallagher smiled. "Wonderful. Elise, dear, that will be all for now. You are excused."

Elise gave the headmaster one more long look. But as she stared, Mrs. Gallagher picked up her Starbucks coffee and sipped from it with a smile. Elise's face pinched in a barely contained rage, and she flew from the room before slamming the door shut behind her.

She ran down the hall and into the main room, where her friends waited for her with eager, hopeful eyes. But their smiles quickly faded when they saw her watery eyes and her splotchy, red face.

"Elise! What happened?" Beth called out.

"Are you okay?" Thomas stepped forward.

"Lisi!" Lily yelled, but Elise couldn't respond to any of them. Not without breaking into sobs and screaming her rage.

Instead, she quickly moved passed them and ran for the front door. The others called for her, and some of the other kids warned her about her chores. She hadn't been inspected by Mrs. Gallagher yet.

But Elise didn't care. She stormed out of the building and sprinted to the only place she felt comfortable. Just as she rounded the corner to the park entrance, she turned toward her bench. But instead of finding the ravens waiting for her on the wall or watching from the trees, she found them squawking and screeching in the air as Brittney and her gang threw rocks at them from the ground.

Elise's eyes widened, and she ran toward them.

"Stop!" she yelled, but the others either didn't hear her at all or ignored her because they kept on laughing, chucking rocks and pieces of the stone wall into the air, aiming for the cawing birds. Just as Elise got close enough, Tyler threw a rock at one of the birds, and it screeched as it toppled to the ground.

"No! Stop it!" She hurtled into Tyler, tackling him onto the grass.

Tyler cried out in surprise as he hit the dirt.

"Leave them alone!" she yelled in his face before looking at the others, who quickly ran in and surrounded her. "These birds have done nothing to you, so leave them be!"

Without her weight fully on him, Tyler pushed her off. Elise landed on her butt in the dirt and looked up to a half circle of snickering, sneering faces.

"What a freak. They're just birds."

"Next, she'll say she can talk to them."

"Are they your friends? I bet they're your only friends."

"Nobody else would willingly choose to be friends with a freak like her."

"Ha! Bet she's got a birdbrain like her friends."

"Birdbrain! Birdbrain!" They all laughed.

Elise tried to stand up and fight her way out, but Raquel shoved her back down. The boys kicked dirt at her, and Elise had to shield her eyes to prevent dirt from getting in them.

"Stop! Stop!" she cried out.

The boys laughed as Raquel spat on her. Elise curled into a tight ball and prayed for the first time in her life—that this would come to an end. She just wanted this to be over. All of it. And as if the heavens above heard her, Brittney screamed, and the kicking stopped. Then the chorus of screams resonated around her.

Elise rubbed the dirt from her eyes, and when she could finally see again, she looked up to find the five kids running in weaving, panicked circles as the ravens dove and pecked and yanked at the kids' hair and clothes.

Two of the ravens dropped rocks on the kids from above, while the other three swooped down and attacked from the sides. Elise watched the kids scream and flail, swatting the birds away until finally, they called a retreat and scattered. Elise stared after them until they disappeared, and that's when the raven with the chipped beak landed on the ground in front of her.

"Hey, it was you that Tyler hit with that rock. Are you okay? Are you hurt?"

The bird did a quick spin and wiggled its head back and forth, as if it understood her and tried to show her that it was okay. Elise smiled and nodded in under-standing.

"Good. I'm glad you're alright." Elise sat up and

looked at them all. All five ravens settled on the ground behind the one with the chipped beak. "I'm glad you're all alright. Truthfully. And, um, thank you for saving me back there. I really appreciate it."

She smiled as they stared at her wordlessly. Even for animals who couldn't speak to her, their company was more than she could've ever asked for. They had saved her from the bullies. They really did care for her more than Mrs. Gallagher or her classmates ever had.

The raven with the chipped beak stepped closer and closer, and soon, it was close enough to touch. But Elise didn't flinch away. It stopped at her feet and dropped a black marble onto the dirt. She eyed it.

"Is this for me?"

The bird bobbed its head. She took that as a yes.

"Thank you." She smiled as she reached for it. But once the marble settled in her palm, it burned her skin like she had just touched a hot stovetop.

Elise cried out in pain as the marble seared her palm. She tried to drop it back onto the ground, but it was stuck to her skin. She peered at it, and found it welding itself into the skin of her palm. She cried out, but the pain didn't go away. Instead, it spread through her wrist, down her arm, and through the rest of her body.

She screamed in pain as she collapsed onto her side. She curled into a ball and moaned as the pain spread and flickered through her. What—what was happening to her? What did that marble do to her?

Elise only remembered burning, searing pain pulsating through her. And then darkness. When she awoke again, the pain was gone, but her hand felt warm, curled into her chest. She squinted in the afternoon light that was shining down on her and found herself still curled up on the grass. She took a shallow breath, testing her body, but nothing burned, nothing ached, nothing hurt.

She extended her fingers slowly, and that's when she saw the marble in her fist again. But this time, it wasn't black; it glowed a deep, vibrant purple. Swirls of it shifted behind the glass, reminding Elise of the oil, water, and glitter experiment she had done in grade school. She used food coloring to dye hers purple, and she could distinctly picture the swirling, glittery purple waves shifting behind the plastic cup that she used.

But this marble, the glow emanating from it on her palm, it almost looked like it was... alive within her.

Small, taloned feet shuffled to a stop in her field of vision. She looked up at the raven standing a mere foot from her head. It was bigger from this angle. It looked darker under the shadow from the sun, more powerful, more beautiful than ever. She found the chip in its beak.

"Hey," she whispered, her voice a low croak, "what did you do to me?"

To her surprise, the raven looked down at her, and a deep voice resonated in her head.

"I gave you the orb."

Elise's eyes widened. "Did you just—?"

The raven bobbed its head yet again. "We have chosen you to be the Keeper of the Orb. It is the Black-wings' most prized and protected possession. And it shall grant you much power."

"You—you can talk to me. In my head. I hear you!" Elise sat up too quickly, suffering through a head rush.

The raven wasn't far, though. "That is one of the powers you've received. You can communicate with ravens now. Not just with the Blackwings, but with all of our kind."

"Okay..." Elise touched her head, feeling for a wound. This wasn't possible; she must have hit her head when Brittney and the others attacked her. But as she ran her hand along her skin, she felt the cool, smoothness of the marble. She gazed at it, molded perfectly into the center of her palm.

"Why—why did you choose me?" she asked.

The raven watched her intently. "We have held onto the orb for many years now, in search of the best human to carry it. We considered you and had been for some time. Ever since you first came upon us at the park that afternoon after your classes. When you sat at that bench and gave us half your sandwich even though your stomach wouldn't stop growling."

Elise remembered her first encounter with the ravens. They perched on the stone wall opposite her bench. She had sat there crying after an especially awful day at school, and the ravens seemed to want to stay and keep her company through her distress.

She thanked them by offering half her sandwich, which she had been looking forward to eating, seeing as how Mrs. Gallagher only sent her to school with a lunchmeat sandwich and a half empty bag of pretzels as punishment for her tardiness to school the day before. But she didn't mind sharing her food, especially if it was among friends. And after the kindness the ravens showed her that day, she was content to share with them. Little did she know, that moment would lead her to where she sat now.

"The Blackwings and I were close to making a decision, when those kids showed up and started throwing rocks at us. When you stepped in to protect us, we knew then that you should be the keeper," the raven finished.

Elise glanced at the others behind him, all watching and listening intently.

"I don't know... if I'm right for this. I mean, what if something happens to it?" she stuttered.

But the ravens didn't look fazed by their decision.

"The decision cannot be undone. We have chosen you, Elise. You are our keeper, and you are a part of the Blackwings."

"What are the Blackwings?"

"Our flock!" A female's voice echoed in her mind. Elise looked behind the chipped beak raven to one of the others and watched her wobble up closer. Her voice was high and scratchy. Elise recognized her as one of twins. She didn't know if they were actually twins, but this raven and the one she left standing behind her had the same blueish, green marking on their left eye.

"The Blackwings is a group of ravens. So, you are part of the Blackwings."

"Oh, okay. That makes sense, I suppose." Elise smiled tightly at her before a realization hit her. "Do you all have names? I'm sorry, I didn't ask."

The bird with the chipped beak nodded and motioned toward the others. The snappy female lifted a wing and hopped a little first.

"I'm Kumi, and that's my twin, Kani."

"I'm Vrukum!" The smaller, thin raven jumped from the back. He was always the first to dive low to the ground, and the first to reach for Elise's snacks, she realized.

She eyed the biggest raven of the group, standing quietly beside Vrukum.

"I am Dolvek."

She nodded with a smile and glanced toward the final member of the group. The bird with the chipped beak stared at her intently, and then his deep voice resonated.

"I am Averin. It is a pleasure to have you join us, Elise."

Elise was speechless as she looked over them all. She had so many questions, and yet none of them seemed important to ask right this minute. For the first time in a long time, she felt relief and a sense of acceptance.

Her chest squeezed with warmth, and she squeezed the marble in her palm. These birds... they really were her friends. They had not only kept her company, but they also listened to her, valued her, protected her, and wanted her to be a part of the Blackwings.

"You will be able to communicate with all the ravens now, but you do also have other abilities with the orb," Averin said evenly.

Elise focused on him. "What can I do?"

"You will be able to talk to and command any raven you so desire, if you choose to do so. You will be able to bend and wield the shadows around you to hide yourself or to mold a weapon."

"A weapon?"

"Yes. Shadow bending allows you to manipulate and move shadows to your will. One thing you can do with that is create shadow weapons to use at your disposal. And when you are finished with them, they simply disappear."

"Wow." Elise glanced at the glowing marble. "That's... a lot of responsibility."

Averin nodded. "We trust you to take care of the orb and to guide the Blackwings in the right direction."

Elise swallowed past the lump in her throat before

looking at him again. "I promise," she said. "I will take good care of it. And all of you, too."

Averin bobbed his head, and the others followed suit as if in a bow.

"Then welcome to the Blackwings."

ELISE SAT ON THE GROUND FOR THE REMAINDER OF the day, not caring about her clothes or about the chill nipping at her skin. She talked to the ravens for hours, learning more about each of them and their personalities, and quickly, she took a liking to this group. She laughed and sighed with them as they all lounged at the park. Until Elise got to the topic of earlier today. She didn't want to relive her humiliating experience, but the boiling rage was never too far when Mrs. Gallagher came to mind.

She told them of her experience, and the ravens scoffed.

"She sounds terrible!" Kumi squawked.

"She is." Elise shook her head.

"We should get back at her!" Vrukum chimed in. "She's shady and terrible, and I'm sure if the public knew about it, they'd want to take her down, too."

Elise eyed the bird as an idea flickered to life in her mind. She glanced at Averin, who seemed to read her mind.

"Do you think it's plausible?" he asked.

Elise nodded casually. "It's not like she's trying too hard to hide her awfulness. One slip up and a call to the press, and we could bring her down for good."

Vrukum bounced with delight. Kumi and Kani wiggled together, cooing and laughing at what was to come. And Dolvek listened intently, but even he took a few steps closer.

Averin gave her a look. "Well, tell us what you need. We are at your disposal."

With that, they spent the rest of the afternoon and early evening plotting the perfect plan to bring down Mrs. Gallagher and an end to her reign.

CHAPTER

FOUR

Elise scrubbed at the dried juice stains on the kitchen counter. Normally, she hated doing chores and resented Mrs. Gallagher for stealing away the limited free time she had on weekends. But today— today was different. She hummed to herself as she picked at a particularly sticky apple juice stain.

Elise could feel the other kids' eyes on her. They watched, waited, and whispered from a distance.

"What is she up to?" they asked each other. "Why is she so happy today? Is something going on? Did her meeting go well yesterday?"

Elise had forgotten all about that terrible meeting.

"Elise." Ms. Augustine approached her with a smile. She sat on the edge of a stool behind the kitchen counter. "How are you doing today?"

Elise smiled as she swiped away at the countertop. "Great, actually. Never better."

"That's great, Elise. It's good to see you so upbeat." Ms. Augustine's smile blossomed, but her suspicion lingered. "Did something happen yesterday? I heard about the meeting that Mrs. Gallagher brought you into."

Elise shrugged. "It wasn't meant to be, that's all. I'm over it already."

Ms. Augustine couldn't even try to hide her surprise. "You... you aren't... upset with her?"

Elise shook her head. "Like I said, it wasn't meant to be. Besides, I'm pretty sure I'm never going to get adopted at this point. I'll probably just age out. But it's fine. I'm not worried about that."

"Oh, Elise. You can't give up hope. That couple yesterday wanted an older child, so there must be more like them. We'll find them for you."

"It's fine, really. I'll be okay. I *am* okay. I'm great!"

"I see that. Did... something else happen yesterday?"

"What do you mean?" Elise scratched at a dried applesauce stain.

"Well, after the meeting, you disappeared all day. And when you came back you were... well, in better spirits."

"Oh. Well, then yes. Something did happen," Elise admitted.

Ms. Augustine tilted her head, waiting for her to continue. Elise smiled wide.

"I made friends yesterday—at the park."

"Oh? Tell me all about them." Ms. Augustine smiled as she settled her head on her propped hand.

"Um, well, they're small and dark and a little mysterious to outsiders. But they're sweet and gentle to me. They welcomed me into their group with open arms, and already, we've made plans to get together again."

"That's great, Elise! I'm so happy for you."

"Thanks." Elise grinned. "I have a feeling they're going to make my life a whole lot better from here on out."

"I'm sure they will." Ms. Augustine took Elise's hand and squeezed her fleshy palm. "Everyone needs friends, Elise. And while I know the kids here are your family, and you take good care of them, it will be nice to have friends your own age on the outside."

Elise nodded, realizing for the first time that she didn't know how old the ravens were exactly. She made a mental note to ask them later.

She threw the dirty rag into the laundry bin and grabbed the broom by the kitchen door. Her last chore was sweeping out the main living area. Thomas had gotten that chore on his list, and strangely enough, Elise's list was easier that day. But she traded Thomas for that one. He had been confused at the time, accusing her of something. He didn't know what exactly—but he knew she would never ask for more or harder chores.

But when Elise said, "fine, then you keep it," he cracked and ended up trading, even if his suspicious gaze lingered on her back, even now.

She hummed to herself as she brushed the dust and dirt into piles from one corner of the room to another. She slowly made her way to the front door, and once there, she opened it wide to brush out the pile she gathered from inside. She left the door wide open.

Elise dropped the broom back in its place and turned at the lightest fluttering of wings. She peered up at the vaulted ceiling and found Averin perched on one of the beams. She smiled, gave him a quick nod, and made her way to Mrs. Gallagher's office.

Mrs. Gallagher required an inspection of their chores every weekend. Because of that rule, she wouldn't be able to go out or do anything else with her new friends until Mrs. Gallagher signed off. On her way to the office, she stopped by to see each of her friends, who were still working away on their own chores. She approached Beth first.

"Hey," she said, stopping just outside of Beth's folded laundry fort stacked all around her.

"Hey," Beth looked up from her half-filled basket, "you're done already?"

Elise nodded. "How are you doing?"

Beth sighed. "I swear, the laundry just increases every week. Do we even own all these clothes? Mrs. Gallagher won't buy us anything new, so where do they all come from? I swear, she just throws her own family's stuff in here so she doesn't have to deal with it."

Elise eyed the leaning piles of neatly folded fabric. "Probably. You know how she is."

Beth sighed yet again. "Yeah, well, I'll be here, slaving over the laundry. Do try to think of me while you're out enjoying the weekend with your new 'friends.'"

Elise raised a brow at her. "You heard already?"

Beth rolled her eyes. "We all heard. You can't fart in a place like this without everyone knowing."

Elise chuckled at the image. "Yeah, I guess you're right."

Beth grew quiet, fiddling with a pink shirt in her hands. "Hey, um, I'm glad you found new friends and all, but... well... don't forget about us, alright?"

Elise stared at her in disbelief. "Beth. No. I would never, okay? Just because I've managed to make some friends outside of here doesn't mean I'm done with you guys. You're my friends, but you're also my family. Okay?"

Beth was slow to nod.

Elise took a step closer. "Okay, Beth?"

Beth gave her a look, but then her eyes softened. "Okay."

"Good. Now quit your crazy talk and come with me." Elise moved farther toward the hallway, and she heard the squeak of Beth's stool scratch against the hardwood floor.

"Wait—what? I can't go anywhere yet. I'm not done."

Elise waved her on. "Don't worry about it. Just come."

"But—"

"Beth—just trust me!" Elise gave her a firm glance, and Beth swallowed. But slowly, she pushed herself up and weaved through her piles of laundry to follow Elise.

Elise picked up Lily and Thomas on the way with similar interactions, and then all four of them were on their way to the main office. Elise knocked on the wooden door, and Mrs. Gallagher's whiny voice echoed from inside.

"Come in."

Elise pushed the door open, and the four of them stepped inside. Mrs. Gallagher eyed them as she sipped from her fresh Starbucks cup. Elise caught sight of the long-printed label on its side and knew, based on the complaining girls at school, that her drink must've cost a small fortune.

"What can I do for you all?" Mrs. Gallagher asked, barely giving them all a second glance.

But Elise didn't stiffen with frustration and anger as she always did in this woman's presence. Her friends waited for her to crack, but Elise was all smiles.

"We've finished our chores for the day and need your inspection, if you have a moment." Elise said, her words dripping with honey.

Mrs. Gallagher set her drink down at the edge of her wide desk with a huff. She pushed herself out of her large, leather chair and walked to the door. "You all finished quickly today and together... Have you been helping each other with your chores again?"

Beth shook her head, Lily and Thomas doing the same. Elise smiled cheerfully.

"No, ma'am. We haven't. We just happened to finish at the same time."

Mrs. Gallagher glanced over her shoulder at her, her eyes narrowed. "Uh-huh. How odd, indeed."

The four of them followed Mrs. Gallagher out of her office, and Elise gazed up at the ceiling, only to find all five ravens perched on a beam. They were ready. Elise smirked.

Mrs. Gallagher made her way to the front of the orphanage first to inspect Elise's work. Elise knew she had cleaned everything spotless, but as usual, Mrs. Gallagher found something to complain about. She crouched down before the ugly suede couch in the open living space and hawked out a laugh as she peered underneath.

"You didn't sweep under the furniture, did you, Elise?"

"I did, ma'am," Elise replied patiently.

Mrs. Gallagher huffed. "Don't lie to me. I can see the evidence with my own eyes. Hand me a broom."

Thomas ran to the kitchen and brought back the broom for the woman. She reached it as far back as she possibly could and dragged out a single dust bunny that Elise had missed in the corner. She pinched it between her manicured claws and held it up to show the kids.

"What does this look like to you, Elise?"

"A dust bunny, ma'am."

"And why would I have found a dust bunny under the couch if you swept under it so thoroughly?"

Elise shrugged. "It was hiding in the corner, easy to miss. It was an honest mistake."

Mrs. Gallagher huffed again as she pushed herself back onto her feet. "Honest mistakes don't get the house clean." She inspected the rest of Elise's chores and found one bump of dried jam at the very back of the countertop and covered with a pile of napkins that Elise had missed. She pointed at a small pile of dust at the foot of the stairs that Elise forgot to sweep out the door with the rest of her dust collection. And did she even try to clean the windows?

Elise told her that window cleaning wasn't on her list that day. Mrs. Gallagher waved her off and said she was adding it. They were so cloudy. How could *anyone* see through them? Her words.

"No wonder it's so dark in here all the time," the headmaster muttered.

Then, satisfied with her own inspection, Mrs. Gallagher moved on to the others. But she didn't have to search long and hard to find something wrong with their work... because they never finished their tasks. Beth's piles of folded laundry sat forgotten, and one pile had even toppled over onto the floor. Thomas was working on cleaning dishes, and in the kitchen sink, sat a pile of unscrubbed, spaghetti sauce-stained plates. And Lily was told to dust the entire main lobby. But as Mrs. Gallagher's finger swept through a layer of dust on the stair banisters, she turned to face the group, her face red and primed to burst.

"Do you think this is funny?" She reared, her eyes wide and bulging.

The others crowded behind Elise, hiding from the headmaster's rage. But Elise stood firm, her smirk settled in place.

"What do you mean?" Elise responded innocently, forcing her voice to sound sweet.

Mrs. Gallagher's nostrils flared, revealing the dark hairs inside. "You never finished your chores! They're only half-done. And what? You all thought that would be acceptable?" The others withered behind her, but

Mrs. Gallagher raged. "Did Elise put you up to this? *Well?*"

They all stared at her in fearful silence. But at Elise's smirk, Mrs. Gallagher stepped closer, inserting herself right in Elise's face. She could practically taste the vanilla coffee on the woman's breath.

"You think you're so funny and above all of us. You think you can do whatever you want here because you'll never get adopted, and you'll age out. But let me tell you right now, that you are not above me. I am the headmaster here, and you are a ward of the state. You are under my control, and until the day that you turn eighteen, you will do as I say, or you will be thrown onto your ass out on the street with nothing to survive but your clothes and your bad attitude." Her hot breath blew in Elise's face. "Do I make myself clear?"

Elise stared into her dark gaze, unfazed and lips sealed. She didn't give her the luxury of answering. Mrs. Gallagher fumed.

"Go." She spat. "All of you go finish your chores, and when you're done, come to me for your next list. Since you feel like wasting my time today, I will do the same in return."

The others started to move, but Elise held up a hand, keeping them in place. Mrs. Gallagher's eyes widened, but Elise didn't relent.

"And *you—*" Mrs. Gallagher raised her voice even further, each word ringing out like a blaring siren. "You will spend the rest of your day watching your friends clean up your mistakes from the timeout chair." She then snorted, amused by her own punishment. "You think you're so tough because of your age, don't you? But even you will sit on the timeout chair, just like all the others."

Lily started to cry behind Elise, and Thomas cleared his throat as he held back tears.

"Mrs. Gallagher—please! Elise didn't mean anything by her actions. It was just—" Beth tried soothing the headmaster, but she wanted none of it.

"Hush, child. Elise will fall on her own sword. Now, get back to work, and Elise—on the chair."

"No."

The headmaster took a step back like she'd pulled out a surprise weapon and startled her with it. The others went silent at her back. Even Lily's sobs quieted to a sniffle.

"What did you say to me?" Mrs. Gallagher tensed, every muscle in her rounded, botoxed body tight and ready to spring.

Elise smirked. "No."

Mrs. Gallagher's perfectly pink lips curled into a snarl. "How *dare* you? I give you everything—*everything*, and *this* is how you treat me?"

The woman's voice rose higher and higher still, but Elise stood there, unbothered and smirking. Ms. Augustine rushed over and tried to wedge herself between the kids and the headmaster.

"Mrs. Gallagher, please, settle down. You're scaring the kids."

"*I'm* scaring the kids?" she howled. "Well, excuse me, Ms. Augustine, but it's *Elise's* fault that I'm like this at all. The gall, the attitude—the ungratefulness!"

Ms. Augustine nudged Elise back, trying to get distance between the women. "I understand your anger, Mrs. Gallagher. But they're only kids. And Elise... Elise didn't mean—"

"Ha!" Mrs. Gallagher pushed the woman aside and grabbed Elise's arm. Lily and Beth cried out as she yanked Elise within inches of her face. She breathed shallowly, each breath reeking of stale coffee and cigarettes. She spat on her face with every word.

"You are the most ungrateful, rude, selfish, and idiotic girl I have ever met. And for what? To prove a point? Do you *really* think you could've gotten you and your friends your freedom sooner with the poor work you did?"

Elise only smiled. "No. And you shouldn't expect that, either."

Mrs. Gallagher raised a brow, but before she could ask what she meant, the ravens attacked.

They swooped down, one after the other and ripped at the hair nestled in a messy bun atop the headmaster's head. She screamed, and the others cried out, too. Ms. Augustine grabbed all the kids and gathered them in the farthest corner of the room as it filled with birds cawing and Mrs. Gallagher's cries of terror.

"What's happening? Who let birds in here?" she shrieked, her arms flailing uselessly around her as she stumbled away from the swooping birds.

She stumbled backward as Kani and Kumi grabbed her hair and yanked in different directions. Vrukum took the opportunity to squawk wildly in her face, his head thrusting forward with his sharp beak. Mrs. Gallagher shrieked, hands flying out wildly to shield herself as she stumbled further back. Her feet shuffled and dragged her backwards as the birds continued with their assault.

But as she drew closer and closer, Elise stuck out her foot and shoved the woman back toward her office. Mrs. Gallagher tripped over herself and cried out as she spun away from the birds. She must have seen the safety of her office, and she ran for it.

But she didn't—she couldn't among the chaos— notice the string that Averin held taut in the doorway. Elise had tied it low on the trim the night before and reinforced it enough so it wouldn't break from her force. Just as planned, Mrs. Gallagher ran through the doorway, her foot caught on the string, and she fell, face first, into her office, clashing against her desk.

She crawled on her hands and knees, and shriveled against the front of her desk as the ravens fluttered and squawked at her from the doorway. As she leaned back and bumped into the wood, the final assault resumed.

Dolvek, perched at the edge of the desk, pushed her giant coffee over the edge, and Elise watched as the milky, icy concoction dripped down her wild nest of hair, over her face, and down her shirt. Mrs. Gallagher screamed, but the kids in the other room cheered.

Ms. Augustine looked among them with wide eyes and an expression of wonder as they high-fived each other and laughed, pointing at Mrs. Gallagher. Elise sidled up to the open doorway and leaned against it with a smirk. Mrs. Gallagher's hair stuck up in every direction, her cheeks were flush with color, and her white blouse was stained a caramel brown and stuck to her skin, showing them all the leopard print bra that she wore underneath. The headmaster stared at the birds, who settled and perched all around Elise.

"You!" Mrs. Gallagher spat coffee from her smeared pink lips.

Elise shrugged as Averin landed on her shoulder. "Your reign here is over, Mrs. Gallagher. Your abuse stops now."

The woman sputtered out more coffee and curled her lips into what surely would have been a splendid insult, but she was cut short when a man's voice resonated from the main room outside the office.

"Hello?"

Elise turned and glanced at the man over her shoulder. He stood just inside the front door. He was dressed in a neatly pressed suit, and his badge hung from his pocket on a chain. Three more men came in behind him; they were decked out in uniforms. Elise smirked.

She wove around the large desk in the center of the office and opened the window. She let her friends hop outside and thanked them for their help before closing the window again.

"Elise—what's going on?" Mrs. Gallagher whispered sharply as she caught sight of the men outside. But Elise stopped in the open doorway and yelled for the men.

"She's over here, officer." The man in the suit caught her gaze, and she smiled sweetly. He moved toward the office.

"What did you *do*?" Mrs. Gallagher spat, clambering to her feet.

Elise smirked at her shocked expression. "I got help. Something you never, ever offered me."

The man in the suit came into the office and took a long look at Mrs. Gallagher. "Hello, ma'am. Are you Cecilia Gallagher?"

Mrs. Gallagher straightened her spine and cleared her throat. "Yes. What is the meaning of this?"

The man, tall, golden, and with fine lines hinting at his age streaking across his face, met Mrs. Gallagher's eyes with an even, serious expression.

"Mrs. Gallagher, I am Detective Roland Miller of the Children's Health and Safety Department. I am here representing the city, county, and state government today."

"Okay...," Mrs. Gallagher's high voice hitched.

"Ma'am, we received a phone call last night about a case of abuse inside your orphanage."

Mrs. Gallagher was quick to respond. "What? That's crazy. None of my children have ever been physically abused. They are loved and well taken care of here."

Detective Miller glanced around the main living area and saw the children's abandoned breakfasts on the counter, consisting of a handful of grapes and crackers for each. He saw the torn cots that the littles—the youngest of them all and mostly toddlers—used in the room off to the side. The room itself was covered in grass, dirt, and dust. And to top it off, his eyes fell on the empty Starbucks coffee cup sitting atop the desk right beside the keys to Mrs. Gallagher's Lexus. He narrowed his eyes at the woman, and she swallowed.

"Hey, kid. Give us the room, alright?" He gave Elise a dry look.

Elise nodded and moved aside for the other officers to step in. She pulled the door closed behind her to the doe-eyed, coffee soaked, and frazzled Mrs. Gallagher. Once the door clicked shut, and Elise heard the lock sound from the inside, she turned to find the other kids watching in stunned, eager silence. She gave them a thumbs up, and they erupted into victorious cheers.

Where did the ravens come from? Were they really ravens, or crows? Who cares! They helped them today. Mrs. Gallagher, the evil witch, was finally going to be dealt with. They should have a party! The chorus of laughter and cheers resonated around her, and Elise smiled warmly at her little family. She caught Ms. Augustine's eyes, and though the woman looked like she had a million questions, she didn't try to ask Elise any of them in that moment. She even smiled herself when the kids started planning the party that they were going to throw that evening.

More and more police officers showed up and started digging through the building. Half of them went upstairs while the other half worked the lower floor. They plucked pieces of clothing, dirt, pictures, toys, and anything and everything they could use in some way was taken out in plastic bags. Some took pictures of the rooms before evidence bags were filled, and a pair of K-9 dogs were even brought in at one point to do a sweep of the house.

Once the evidence were all picked and bagged, the interviews began. Officers took kids in every direction and asked them questions about their experience at the orphanage. Everyone was quiet and shy at first, but as one started talking, they all started spilling the truth.

Elise sat down with a balding man, with a gut so round that it looked fake, like one of those suits they used for movies. He asked her question after question, and Elise happily answered him.

"Your statement today," the man finished, "it's honest and true to the best of your ability?"

Elise nodded firmly. "Every word of it."

The man left with the others, and in their wake, sat

an empty, quiet house. That was, until two officers showed up with forty bags filled to the brim with McDonald's Happy Meals. The kids went crazy, reaching and grabbing for the food. They stuffed the greasy food into their mouths and moaned at the pleasure it gave them.

It had been… well, Elise couldn't remember the last time they had been treated to any kind of food that wasn't prepackaged or snacks from the store. She slowly chewed on her fries, letting the salty grease settle on her tongue. She watched the younger kids run around in the empty house and play with their new McDonald's toys, a smile ingrained on her face.

Soon enough, the door to the office finally opened, and they all glanced up to find Mrs. Gallagher being led out in handcuffs by one of the officers. The other two carried out sagging stacks of binders, filled to the brim with papers. The man in the suit followed behind. He pulled Ms. Augustine aside and spoke to her in hushed tones while the kids all danced and laughed at Mrs. Gallagher. She glared at them all, but she didn't even try to bite back because the officer at her back tightened his grip and shoved her outside.

THE KIDS ALL WENT TO BED GIDDY AND GIGGLING that night. All the fear and anxiety had vanished with

Mrs. G, and in its place, there was a bright future. Once the others had fallen asleep, Elise snuck out of her room and searched for Ms. Augustine downstairs. She found her cleaning up the mess of Mrs. Gallagher's office.

"So?" Elise asked from the doorway.

Ms. Augustine nearly jumped out of her skin at the sight of the teenage girl. "Dear Lord, Elise. Don't sneak up on me like that."

Elise chuckled before taking a seat on one of the chairs in front of the desk.

"What now?"

Ms. Augustine plopped down across from her, but she looked out of place in the hulking leather chair that Mrs. Gallagher used.

She sighed. "I don't know. Apparently, Mrs. Gallagher's poor treatment of all of you wasn't the only crime she committed, and she's being investigated by the police. Detective Miller left me in charge until they can find a suitable replacement."

Elise had to reel in her smirk at the woman's tired and strained expression. "Hey, that's okay. You've worked here for years. You know all of us and what is required to run the orphanage. You can do this."

Ms. Augustine gave her the tiniest of smiles. "Thank you, really. It's all just a bit... sudden."

"Is the government going to give you back any of the money that Mrs. G stole?"

Ms. Augustine eyed her. "How did you—" She

shook her head. "You're smarter than you think, Elise. And entirely too observant for your age."

Elise smiled at that. "It's not like she tried to hide it."

"Yes, well, you'd be right with that." Ms. Augustine sighed. "To answer your question, yes. The government is giving me a substantial bonus to take care of all of you in the meantime."

"So... Thomas can finally get new shoes for school?"

"Yes."

"And Beth can get a yearbook this year?"

"Yes."

"And we can all stop eating grapes and stale snacks for meals?"

Ms. Augustine chuckled. "Yes. To everything. I may not be perfect, and I'm definitely going to need time to adjust, but I will do the best I can to make you all happy. You deserve that much after that woman—" She shook her head. Kind and sweet Ms. Augustine couldn't even say the evil witch's name. Elise chuckled to herself.

"Oh, and I meant to tell you. You can thank your friends for me."

Elise's smile dropped, and she stared at the woman before her. "What—what do you mean?"

Ms. Augustine wasn't dumb, though. She smiled knowingly.

"I don't know how or why, and I won't ask. Just... thank them for me, will you? For all of us."

Elise watched her, and something in her chest fluttered. A warmth spread throughout her, and for the first time in a very long time, she was happy. Ms. Augustine squeezed her hand like she had so many times before, and Elise squeezed hers right back.

"Get to bed. You've had a long day," she said.

Elise stood up, but she stopped in the doorway. She took one more look at the dark bags under Ms. Augustine's eyes, and she couldn't help herself.

"Hey, for the record, I think you'd be a great headmaster."

Ms. Augustine's smile cracked, and her eyes welled with tears, but she didn't let them fall. She nodded, and Elise took that as her cue. She went up the stairs and down the hall to her bedroom. She lied in bed in the dark amongst her friends and swiftly drifted off to a chorus of slow, restful breaths. She smiled to herself and found herself eager for the next day, a feeling she hadn't felt for as long as she could remember.

CHAPTER

FIVE

ELISE MET WITH THE RAVENS THE NEXT DAY AFTER school.

After such an eventful day at the orphanage, Elise was riding high on buzzing energy. She made plans in her own mind to stand up for herself at school. To fight back against Brittney and her gang of thugs, and to make the teachers see their mistakes. Elise stepped through the front door of the school that day with a shield of pride and only a little imagined courage.

But as she stepped inside her classroom, she found it quiet. Everyone mumbled and whispered amongst themselves, and Brittney's crew... was without Brittney.

It turned out that Brittney was going to be absent because of some "family emergency" at home. Elise snickered to herself.

Wonder what that emergency is, she thought dryly.

The rest of Brittney's gang left her alone all day. The boys at her back were quiet, and Raquel at her side, kept her eyes and her hands to herself. Elise nearly bubbled over in happiness, and the icing on the cake? A crow perched on a tree branch right outside the classroom window during class and tapped on the glass with its beak. Everyone else thought it was funny, but one look at Brittney's gang, and Elise saw the flinches and the red cheeks. Elise couldn't stop her smirk. Her ravens had done well.

"So, did they do anything to you yesterday?" Elise asked as she sat on her bench in the park.

The ravens looked at each other as if communicating silently before Kani finally answered. "No, they didn't bother us at all. It was nice, actually, since they usually harass us whenever we go near their territory."

Elise was both surprised and relieved to hear this. She had been really worried that the bullies would do something bad to her friends, but it seemed like they had just left them alone. Maybe things were finally starting to look up for them.

"That's great! I'm glad they didn't do anything to you," Elise said with a smile.

Elise breathed a sigh of relief and gave the ravens an appreciative pat on the head. She was glad they were safe for now, and that the bullies had finally left them alone. But she also knew they weren't out of the woods yet, and that they'd have to be careful from now on. She just hoped that things would start getting better from here.

Elise pulled out a packet of peanut butter crackers that she had left aside at lunch. She handed one to each of them, careful to avoid Kani and Kumi, who were already guzzling theirs down. Dolvek picked quickly and happily at his, while Vrukum swallowed his whole. Averin accepted his but didn't touch it. Instead, he asked Elise about the aftermath of their victory.

Averin looked around at his team, all of them staring back at him expectantly. He had been quiet since they succeeded in their first mission together—rescuing Elise from the clutches of the "evil witch," Mrs. Gallagher. Elise had been a great help, and he was glad to have her on the team. But what now? This was only their first job together, and it had gone smoothly. It seemed wasteful to stop there.

"What's next?" Averin asked quietly, meeting each of their gazes in turn before turning his attention back to Elise. She seemed to understand what he was asking, and she smiled softly before answering.

"We keep doing what we do best—helping people," she said confidently, her blue eyes bright.

Averin felt a warmth in his chest at her words, and he nodded in agreement. He was ready for whatever came next. Whatever it was, he knew he could count on his team to help him get through it.

Elise beamed and broke the last cracker into pieces. She handed out the pieces to each of them, patting them on the head before pushing herself off the bench.

"Where are you going?" Vrukum squawked.

Elise shrugged. "A walk around the park, I guess. Want to join me?"

The ravens followed her up and down sidewalks, flying overhead as she walked. Elise thought about Averin's words as she strolled, and an idea popped into her head. She thought about all the other orphanages in the city. All the other kids who had been forgotten, left alone, and abused, just like her. She wanted to help them, too.

Maybe this was the start of something new for her. Maybe she could make a difference in the world, just like her team was doing. She still had a lot to learn, but she was ready to do whatever it took.

Elise stopped at a water fountain in the center of the path. The birds perched on the metal before her.

"Do you think we can do this again? Righting the wrongs of abusive headmasters and run-down orphanages?" she asked. "There are still a lot of kids we can help in other orphanages."

The ravens all exchanged looks before nodding slowly.

"Why not? We did it once; we can do it again!" Vrukum cawed.

"Let's do it!"

"Yeah!" Kani and Kumi cheered.

Dolvek looked at her quietly, but even he nodded in agreement.

That left Averin. It was his idea to begin with, but Elise was most nervous about his response. Averin stared at her with those glowing eyes of his, and Elise faltered. But Averin dipped his head in the smallest of bows.

"We will help you, Elise."

Elise's eyes welled with tears, which she wiped away with the sleeves of her sweatshirt. The birds all jumped and cawed at her, but she laughed, waving them off.

"I'm fine, I'm fine. Just... happy to have you all in my life."

The ravens cooed at her, and she couldn't hide her smile. It bubbled out of her, warm and inviting. They all made their way back to the bench that they normally sat at and began plotting a new plan.

Elise would use her power, and with the Black-wings and any others around the city, they could all do exactly what they had done at her orphanage. They could bring down these terrible, abusive, and power-hungry adults, and they could help the children who were stuck under their thumb. They would make a difference. But first, they had to decide on a target. Elise needed Beth and her quick, research-based mind for that.

"I'll go with Beth to investigate the situation of the next orphanage. That way, we can get a good look of the inside and map out the entire place. It'll be easier to execute the plan if we have a map." Elise told them her next step.

"Good idea," Kumi said, before taking flight. The sun was dipping, and the bright light of day was disappearing. Elise needed to get back soon.

The other ravens followed Kumi, each one promising their help and giving Elise support before fluttering off to the trees. Averin was the last to go, and he lingered.

"Talk to your friend, and let us know the plan."

"I will," Elise replied.

"And be safe, you two. We won't be far if you need any help."

Elise stared at her newest friend and grinned. "Thank you, Averin. For everything."

Averin nodded. "Get yourself home before it gets too dark. We shall talk tomorrow." And then he, too, followed the others.

Elise made her way back to the orphanage, all smiles and glee. She had her ravens, and they had her.

They would never be alone again. Once she returned, she found Beth and pulled her up to their bedroom. She locked the door behind them, and the two talked about the events of the previous day.

Elise admitted to her best friend that she had been the one who orchestrated the attack with the ravens. Beth was a bit... confused at first—mostly about the ravens part—but she didn't seem surprised to know that Elise had been the one to make the plan and take down Mrs. Gallagher.

Beth shook her head in amazement. "You're so brave, Elise. I don't know if I could do what you did."

Elise shrugged. "It wasn't really that brave. I just wanted to help the other kids. They are my family, and they deserve better."

Beth was in disbelief, but she didn't question it much more than that. She knew Elise was powerful, and she could probably do some serious damage if she wanted to. But Beth had never seen her use her power in such a way before. It was daunting, but impressive.

"So, what's next?" Beth asked.

Elise thought for a moment. She knew that there were other orphanages like the one they had just attacked. Ones that were doing just as much, if not more, damage to the children inside them. She also knew that they were vulnerable. Mrs. Gallagher had been abusing and neglecting the children for years, and no one had ever done anything about it.

But now, things would be different.

"We keep doing what we do best. We take down the orphanages, and we help kids like us." This was only the beginning. With her powers and the help of the Blackwings, they could give hope to the orphans of their city, and shine a light on what's really happening behind the scenes.

Beth was taken aback by Elise's words. "Are you sure? I mean, this is a *lot* of responsibility."

Elise nodded confidently. "We can do this. But I need your help in finding the next target."

"I'll go online and check some sites. See if I can find any that match the profile we're looking for," Beth said as she got up to leave.

Elise watched her get the laptop that Ms. Augustine had provided for her the very next day after Mrs. Gallagher was taken away. She had needed it for school for so long, but the evil witch wouldn't grant her one. Beth was smart and quick-witted, but she couldn't live up to her full potential because of Mrs. Gallagher's greed. But now, she was unstoppable.

The two of them got to work, spending hours researching orphanages, looking for ones that were doing the most harm to their children.

It was hard work, but Elise and Beth were determined. When the light outside their window had disappeared entirely, and the faint glow of the street lamp was their only means of seeing, they decided that Ravensford Orphanage would be their next target. It was the closest orphanage to theirs, and it had a questionable reputation. Even if, externally, it appeared like a homey, blue house, inviting to all.

"Now, we're all set," Elise said as she grinned at Beth. "Are you ready?"

Beth felt a little nervous. This wasn't exactly the safest mission for the both of them. They didn't know what could happen along the way. But she trusted Elise enough to agree to go.

"Yes, let's do this." She smiled, trying to muster confidence. "All we have to do is make a map so that we know where everything is. It looks like the open hours are from one in the afternoon until four. We should be able to get a good look around then." Beth replied eagerly, her eyes shining with excitement.

The girls spent the rest of the night plotting out their route on paper and making sure they knew exactly when they needed to make it to the orphanage. They were both so excited about their adventure that they could barely sleep a wink.

The next day, they woke up early and set out for Ravensford Orphanage.

CHAPTER

SIX

THE NEXT DAY, ELISE AND BETH DECIDED TO MAKE their way to Ravensford, their next target.

"I wonder how big it is," Beth pondered as they walked. "And what the kids are like."

"It can't be that different from ours," Elise chimed in. "I mean, all orphanages have to follow the same rules and regulations."

"I hope not," Beth said. They turned a corner and

saw the orphanage in the distance. It was much bigger than their orphanage. "Wow."

"There must be other orphanages in the city, with kids experiencing the same horrible things that we did," Elise whispered as they walked around the streets, looking at the buildings around them.

"I bet there are," Beth agreed. "And we'll find them."

Eventually, they found themselves outside of Ravensford. It looked so nice from the outside, with its bright blue walls and cheerful decorations. But as they got closer, they could see the cracks in the façade.

The front door sat at a lilt, surely letting too much heat out and too much cold air in during the winter time. There was more than one broken window on the upper floors, there was a layer of soot and grime across the side of the building, and trash littered down the alleyway, too.

But the public didn't see that side of Ravensford; they saw the bright blue exterior and thought, *Those poor kids! At least they have a nice place to stay until they get adopted!*

But Elise and Beth knew. Looks could be deceiving. Mrs. Gallagher had shown them that much.

"I don't like the look of this," Beth said, her voice trembling.

The plan was that Beth and Elise would pretend to be orphans in order to get inside, get a feel for Ravensford, and draw a map of its interior.

"Beth, we agreed on this," Elise replied, her patience thinning as her own anxiety pressed in.

"Yeah, but look how big it is!" Beth waved at the building. "And what if we step two feet inside, and they recognize us?"

"How would they recognize us? We live on the other side of the city."

"You know what I meant. They could take one look at us and know we don't belong here, and then our whole plan and everything will fail before it's begun."

Elise took a steadying breath. "Look, it's going to work, okay? Trust me. A place like this has kids going in and out every day. They can't keep track of them all. And you're right—it's huge! But while that means we will have more ground to cover, it also means that there are more kids and more blind spots to cover us."

Beth eyed her, and Elise tilted her head.

"Beth?"

Beth sighed. "Fine. Okay. Let's go."

The two of them stepped inside, holding their breath. Elise didn't know what to expect, even after her morale boosting speech to Beth. But when she stepped inside and saw everything just as it had been at her orphanage only *bigger*, her breath rushed out of her in a *whoosh*.

The two of them wandered around for a bit, trying to get a sense of the place. It was bigger than their orphanage, with more kids. But it also felt colder. More sinister. Beth took notes in her notebook of the pathways while drawing a map underneath.

She followed Elise without pause and let her lead the way. They wove up and down every hall and peeked into each room to get a better idea of what they were dealing with. Some of the kids around them ignored them completely, but others gave them narrowed glances. They didn't recognize them, and they wouldn't. But as long as they stayed silent and didn't raise the alarms, Elise didn't mind.

"I don't think this is going to be easy," she whispered to Beth as they passed the main living area and rushed past a group of young kids gathered together on the couch. They all looked up at them and gave them a perplexed look, but their lips stayed sealed when one of the adults walked by behind them. "They're scared."

Beth nodded. "We'll figure it out.."

They kept walking, looking for anything that could help them. But it was difficult. They didn't want to do anything that would draw attention to themselves. They went past the areas where potential adopters would see them, which were clean, pristine, and decorated with pictures of smiling children.

And then they explored the hidden depths of Ravensford, the areas not seen by the public. They went down into the dank basements and wound through the hallways. Everywhere they looked, there were signs of neglect: rats crawling over piles of trash, children with bruises and scars, cold rooms with no heat.

"I can't believe this place is allowed to stay open," Beth hissed. "It's torture!"

Elise nodded grimly. "We're going to change that. We'll find the kids who are in the worst situations, and we'll give them hope."

Hope. It was a new word to Elise. Before this, she would have been satisfied with peace or independence, or maybe just being left alone. But after the downfall of Mrs. Gallagher, she wanted more for her little family, and she wanted more for others who were suffering in the same way. These kids needed hope.

They kept exploring, and eventually, they found a group of kids who were huddled in a corner of the staircase, trying to keep warm. Their clothes were tattered, and their eyes were sunken.

Beth stifled a cry. "How could they—?"

Elise pushed her up the stairs, trying to keep her eyes down from the huddled kids. She would help them—she *would*. But she needed more time. This had to be done right. They stumbled up to the second floor and came upon a room in the very back corner of the hall. Elise opened the door and found a dark room, the windows inside covered with trash bags to keep the light out.

"What is that?" Beth asked. She carefully walked inside. But as her friend fumbled for a light switch, she tripped on something in the center of the room. "Ouch!"

"Are you okay?" Elise turned in the dark and could barely make out Beth crouched down.

"Is that... a chair?"

Elise squinted her eyes in the dark, hoping to see what the metal clanking sound was, and saw what looked like restraints attached to the armrests and at the base of the chair. There was also a rolling table nearby with syringes and other cold metal tools on it. A wave of nausea washed over her.

Elise pictured herself strapped onto the chair, screaming for help as the adults pricked her with needles and syringes, injecting her with who knows what. She could feel the cold metal burn her skin, see the fear in her eyes as she struggled against the restraints.

"Elise?" Beth's voice snapped her out of her trance. "What is it? What do you see?"

She shook her head to clear it and looked around the room. There were more chairs like the one she had just seen, and tables with medical equipment. It looked like a torture room.

"This is...," Elise muttered, her voice trembling.

"What was that metal sound?" Beth asked, fear creeping into her voice.

Elise swallowed hard and tried to keep her voice steady. "Don't worry." She lied as she pushed it away to the corner. "It's just a table." She had never seen anything like this before, but she knew that it was bad. Really bad. And she didn't want to linger.

They were about to leave the room when, suddenly, an adult came down the hallway and stepped inside. He looked like he was looking for something, as he shuffled through objects in the cabinets against the far wall of the room.

Elise hid herself and Beth in the shadows using her powers. She didn't know how she did it, but she could feel that purple orb in her hand flickering with energy as she brought it to life. She peered out at the man through the blanket of darkness surrounding them and could feel Beth's eyes flickering on her, too. She ignored them for now.

Her heart raced as the man got closer and closer in his search for whatever he needed.

Please don't find us, she thought frantically. *Please!*

But then the man turned back to the cabinets, muttering.

"What do you think he's looking for?" Beth whispered.

Elise shook her head as they continued to observe the man from afar. But she had an idea of what he was up to. Elise didn't say anything to Beth. She didn't want to scare her more than she already was.

Beth shivered beside her. "Do you think he'll find us?"

"I don't know," Elise whispered, trying not to let

the fear show in her voice. "But we need to get out of here."

"Ah... ha!" The man finally held up a silver metallic tool in his hand, but not before Elise and Beth saw a sinister smirk on his face. Elise's blood boiled.

"Do you think he would hurt us?" Beth asked, her voice trembling.

"Yeah," Elise admitted. "Maybe. If we get caught. We need to be careful."

Elise and Beth were horrified by what they had seen in Ravensford so far. Elise was done—she had seen enough to last a lifetime. But she knew they had to do something to help the kids who were being tortured there. It wouldn't be easy, but it was necessary.

It took everything in her being to not snap on the intruder—she could feel the anger and frustration coiling inside of her like a snake, ready to strike. But she restrained herself; it wouldn't do either of them any good if she got caught.

Thankfully, the intruder soon left, leaving Elise and Beth alone and able to leave the torturous room. Elise fumed as they made their way out of the room. She could barely contain her anger, imagining the kids tied up and picked at like some kind of experiment. If the adult involved was anything like Mrs. Gallagher, they probably used this room as a form of punishment. Elise couldn't even imagine.

"Let's get out of here," Elise whispered, grabbing Beth by the arm as she made her way out of the room.

They quickly shut the door behind them, trying not to make too much noise.

But as they ran to the end of the hall, they ran into an older boy around Elise's age. He was tall and willowy, like the weeping willows she so loved at the park. His skin looked like it would normally be a golden brown, but it appeared pale and suspiciously sickly. His cheeks were thin, and his arms even thinner, but his eyes were a bright, thunderous gray.

"So, what are you doing here all by yourselves?" the boy asked, eyeing the darkroom behind Beth and Elise.

The two girls exchanged a nervous glance before Elise answered. "We just wanted to take a look around. We're new here and haven't explored the house."

The boy didn't seem convinced. He scratched his arm incessantly as if he had fleas or something. "You sure about that? I don't remember seeing you around before."

Elise steeled her spine and put on her best air of confidence. Even after everything that she had found and everything that she had witnessed—even the boy in front of her, yet another example of Ravensford's abuse.

"We're new. I already told you. But we're going back downstairs now, so excuse us." Elise gently pushed past the boy, dragging Beth behind her. But she stopped halfway down the stairs at his last warning.

"You guys better be careful and not get caught by the headmaster. Or you'll end up in there, like me."

He unveiled his arms, scarred and inflamed from needle marks and scratches, some new and others faded and bruised yellow with age. Elise's eyes widened at the sight.

"This place is a madhouse. You can't trust anyone here. Not even the teachers."

The boy's words sent a shiver down Elise's spine. "I'm sorry," she whispered, her face going pale as she stared at his arms. "We didn't mean to—"

"It's okay," the boy interrupted. "Just be careful from now on, yeah?"

Elise pushed Beth further down the steps before she turned and took the boy's hands in hers.

"This will all be over soon. We'll come back for you," Elise promised.

The boy looked at her, his gray eyes red-rimmed and swimming with doubt. But he nodded, and with that, Beth and Elise made their escape. They raced down the steps and rounded the corner, but to their dismay, the exit was blocked by the headmaster and an adult talking about what to do with the other kids inside the orphanage. Beth and Elise looked at each other. How were they going to get out?

The older boy came up behind them with a worried look on his face.. "You guys need to go. Now."

Beth and Elise didn't need to be told twice. But

they had to figure out how to lead the adults away from the exit. The boy gave them a reassuring look.

"Don't worry, I'll distract them so you guys can run. Got it?" He quickly told them as he spied on the adults from the railing of the stairs.

Beth and Elise nodded silently. The boy moved.

He saw the headmaster coming and quickly ran toward her, bumping into her intentionally.

"Orion! What are you—" She glared at him and lifted her hand to hit him when he bolted in the opposite direction from the girls. The headmaster and the other adult followed, calling for him to stop.

When they saw the adults run, Elise and Beth made their move. They sprinted through the entrance of Ravensford, Elise's anger growing with every step. After they bolted out the door and turned down an alley across the street, they saw a group of kids being dragged in by two adults. One of the kids was crying, and Elise could feel the tremors of his fear lodged in her own throat.

She turned to Beth, her anger boiling over. "We have to do something. We can't just stand here and do nothing."

Beth nodded, her eyes determined. "We'll find a way. But we have to come up with a plan first."

Elise itched to act now. To call upon the Black-wings and have them meet her at the front door. She wanted to take Ravensford by storm and let these kids sleep peacefully tonight, just as she had. But Beth was right. They needed a plan. That was the only way they could help these kids.

"Come on," Beth whispered, tugging on Elise's arm as they made their way back onto the streets.

Elise felt guilt crawl into her chest and block her throat as she thought of what that boy had done for them. She knew what horrors that boy faced. He was most likely going to get caught and end up getting punished even more than he already had. But she was also grateful for his help. Without him, they would never have escaped. Beth looked like she was thinking the same thing.

Stay strong, Elise prayed to the wind. They'd be back for him.

BACK AT THEIR ORPHANAGE, THEY FOUND THEIR friends playing a board game with some of the other kids in the main living area. They called for Beth and Elise to join them, but the two girls waved them off, feigning fatigue from their day out. They made their way up to the bedroom and locked the door behind them. Elise moved for her bed, giving only one look out the single window.

But the one look gave her a glimpse of black fluttering of feathers. Averin flew by her window as if signaling her to open it. Elise let Averin inside, not without noticing Beth's wide gaze.

Averin landed on her bed and perched there. He eyed Beth suspiciously, but Elise waved at her. "She's my friend. I trust her."

Averin cooed at Beth, but his voice was clear in Elise's mind. "Any friend of yours, is a friend of ours. Please tell your friend my name."

Elise grinned tightly, the first glimpse of a smile she had all day. "Beth, this is Averin. He's one of my new friends."

"Is he—was he one of the birds that took down Mrs. Gallagher?"

Elise nodded, and Beth stared at Averin in wonder. Elise didn't know how she thought her friend would react to the raven, but she wasn't afraid or weirded out by him at all.

"Thank you for your help, Averin," Beth started. "We all sincerely appreciate it."

Averin bobbed his head, acknowledging her gratitude, but then he turned his eyes to Elise again.

"I like her," he said flatly.

Elise chuckled. "I like her, too."

Elise plopped onto her bed and stretched wide to release all the tension that had coiled her muscles into a tight mess that day. But as her arm rubbed on the wooden frame, it caught on a splinter. Elise hissed as she yanked her arm away, finding a scratch on her skin.

It was nothing serious, but suddenly, the image of the boy at Ravensford popped into her mind. His scratched and bruised arms, his thin figure, his hopeless expression—

"This is ridiculous!" Elise exclaimed, her voice trembling with rage. "We can't just sit here and do nothing while the kids at Ravensford are tortured."

Beth gave her friend a sympathetic look, but at Averin's tilted head, she explained everything. Their trip to Ravensford, their exploration of its insides, the abuse and torture room that they saw around every corner, and the boy who helped them escape.

Averin nodded solemnly, his yellow eyes bright in the darkness of the room.

"What are we going to do?" Elise threw up her hands, the boiling rage simmering in her bones.

"We're going to get them out of there, right? We have to," Beth stated firmly. "We can do it, just like you did it here, Elise. With your friends' help..."

Elise looked to Averin and found him nodding in agreement.

"Those kids are living in terrible conditions, by the sound of it. If they are suffering a fraction of what you did, Elise, then I think we should help save them."

"Really? You'd help me again?" Elise stuttered.

Averin's eyes brightened. "You are one of us now. We take care of our own."

Something in Elise's chest clenched, and she had to swallow past the lump in her throat. She nodded, trying to distract herself from the warm, bubbling feelings in her chest. She glanced at Beth.

"You have the maps you drew?"

Beth pulled out her notebook and set it on the bed. They all peered at her notes and studied the drawn maps, and in the wee hours of the night, Averin flew off to tell the rest of the Blackwings their plan.

CHAPTER

SEVEN

Ravensford Orphanage was shut down two days later.

Their plan went smoothly, and Elise, Beth, and the ravens watched the downfall from across the street. They sat on a park bench, and they watched the cops infiltrate the blue monster of a building. They watched the headmaster get walked out in handcuffs. They watched the children of the orphanage stare with wide, bulbous eyes. And then—they heard the cheers.

Elise smiled to herself the whole walk back to her own orphanage. And there, she sat in the main living area with the others and watched the evening news after dinner. Ms. Augustine had purchased a TV as one of her first post-Mrs. Gallagher gifts to the kids. She let them watch TV, play games, and have a certain amount of hours of screen time each day.

The kids loved it, and many had never seen a TV before then.

In the evenings, however, when all the younger kids were put to bed, the older kids sat to watch the news with Ms. Augustine. Tonight, the headline read *Ravensford Orphanage - EXPOSED* in big, bold print.

Elise watched the video tapes taken earlier in the day of the exact moment the police showed up to the orphanage. The cries and yells erupting from inside the walls as the newscasters stepped inside, too. They panned around the living space, and the main woman —Alexa Riley—noted the faults of the place, just as Elise and Beth had days before. While the exterior was bright and welcoming, it was all a façade. A mask to hide the dark interior.

Alexa had the camera panned over the wide-eyed faces of the children, all huddled to the side and watching the scene play out in confusion... and maybe a little fear. She heard murmurs of "the ravens," "that *girl*," and "what now?"

And then the door to the headmaster's office slammed open, the camera shot up, and out walked the headmaster. His head hung low, and he turned his splotchy, red face from the camera as the police officer behind him pushed him forward, out the front door, and into the closest cop car. And then, Elise saw exactly what she heard—the hush of the children exploding into wild, victorious cheers.

Alexa interviewed a couple of the kids and had them recount their stories of the orphanage and its horrors to the camera. All the while, shots of footage played at the corner of the screen, making its way through the orphanage, covering the bottom floor, and then up to the second floor. It exposed all the cracks unseen by the public, and showed the world the horrid conditions that the children were kept in.

And then—as one little girl talked about "the *room* at the end of the hall," the wandering camera stopped outside the wooden door at the end of the hall on the upper floor. Elise held her breath, remembering her discovery of the room, the tools stored there, the cold, dark feeling, and her almost encounter with the head-master himself.

The man had smiled when he found a tool. That red, splotchy, embarrassed face was gleeful in the moment. He *enjoyed* spreading hurt and terror among the children who could not stand up for themselves. Elise's fists clenched, her nails biting into her palms. But she was brought back to the present when Beth laid her warm, soft hand on top of hers. Elise looked up at her friend and found her smiling gently.

"We got him. It's over," she whispered.

Elise's fist slowly loosened, and she squeezed Beth's hand. She took a steadying breath and turned back to the TV, where the camera footage had stopped and, instead, remained on Alexa.

"Well, as tragic and horrendous as this situation was for all these children, today was a win. It may still be early, but petitions have already been made, calling for Ravensford to be shut down altogether. If that happens, the children will be dispersed among the other orphanages in the city, where hopefully, they will be in much better hands." She smiled at the camera before turning her attention to a boy standing slightly off-screen. She extended her microphone out, and the camera shifted. Elise's eyes widened.

It was the boy from before! The one who had helped her and Beth when they were scouting Ravensford. While still pale, thin, and bruised, he beamed. Something in Elise's chest squeezed at his pearly smile. It was bright and luminous like the sun. She couldn't believe the darkness of Ravensford tamping down that light for so long.

"Hello, what is your name?" Alexa smiled, her face clear and vibrant, but lacking any smile lines.

The boy leaned into the mic. "My name's Orion."

"Nice to meet you. Orion, are you nervous about Ravensford potentially being shut down?"

Orion smiled even brighter. "I am ecstatic about the possibility."

Alexa huffed out a breathy laugh. "You do know you and all the other children will have to be rehomed, right?"

Orion nodded. "Ma'am, while I will miss some of my friends here, I would rather us be apart and know that each and every one of us is safe and happy than stay here together and suffer. Ravensford is a madhouse, and it deserves to crumble."

"Wow, powerful words from someone so young."

It was Orion's turn to scoff. "I'm seventeen, ma'am. And I've helped to practically raise many of the kids here."

Alexa smiled, that look plastered onto her wrinkleless face. "I see. Then I wish you all the best, Orion."

"Thank you."

"Is there anything else you'd like to say before we go?"

Orion turned his gaze to the camera, his eyes dark and shining even in the dimness of the receded sunlight. Elise felt like he was looking right at her, like he could see her through the screen. She swallowed.

"I'd like to thank Ravenkin for saving us all today. She didn't have to and, truthfully, most people wouldn't because many just don't care about the forgotten kids of the city. But she—she cares."

The murmurs around the cameramen grew quiet; even the sirens and shouts of the police in the background seemed to pause. Alexa leaned in closer to Orion.

"I'm sorry, you said Ravenkin? What exactly is that?"

"A girl who can control and communicate with the ravens. She's one of them. She was the one who came in, took out our headmaster today, and exposed him to the police. And I imagine she called you, too."

Alexa eyed the cameraman, and Elise could hear a voice mumble from behind the camera, "We did get an anonymous tip."

She turned back to Orion, her smile slipping into something more serious.

"You say this girl can talk to birds? And she came into your orphanage?"

"*Ravens.* And yes, she came right through the front door, she took out the headmaster within moments, and with help from the black birds. And then, when the headmaster was helpless and unguarded, the cops came in." Orion smiled more to himself. "She saved us. She kept her promise."

"You met her before?"

"I don't know for sure. But a girl told me she would come back for me, and days later, Ravensford was brought to its knees." Orion shrugged, seeming to remember the camera before him. "Anyway, if she's watching, I want to thank her. Thank you, Ravenkin. I will forever be grateful to you."

Alexa's brow furrowed, and the silence after Orion

finished dragged on. The sound of a throat being cleared behind the camera caught her attention and brought her back. She visibly shook herself and straightened as Orion stepped back out of view.

"Well, you heard it here first. A girl who talks to ravens exposed the horror house called Ravensford today, with flapping, black birds at her aid. It sounds to me like the city has a new superhero." She chuckled before she gave the camera one final salute. "Whoever you are—the city thanks you, Ravenkin. And now—back to you, Jeff."

The screen switched back to the news studio, and a gray-haired man started talking about the upcoming increase in gas prices. Elise tuned out as Beth glanced at her. She raised a brow with the smallest of knowing smiles.

"Ravenkin, huh? It's catchy."

Elise shook her head with a smile of her own. "I'm no superhero."

Beth shrugged. "The city seems to think so."

"The news is just grabbing onto another catchy headline. A girl who can talk to ravens? Yeah, right. They'll forget about me in a week."

"If you say so," Beth teased.

All the other kids around them murmured and laughed, talking about the story that sounded so eerily similar to the exposure of their own orphanage. Lily and Thomas turned around from their cushions on the floor and grinned at the older girls.

"Did you see, Elise? That orphanage got saved by ravens, too! Can you believe it?" Lily squealed.

"Maybe Ravenkin was the one who saved us, too. I mean, how many people do you know that can talk to ravens?" Thomas chimed.

"None!"

"Exactly. So maybe Ravenkin came here, too. Maybe she was the one who got Mrs. Gallagher taken away!"

"Do you think it was her? Really, really?" Lily's eyes widened with uncontained hope.

Beth gave Elise a sideways glance, her smile lingering. Elise sat up straighter with a sigh.

"You didn't see her, though. Maybe the ravens just... you know, flew inside the door that day. I did leave it open by accident when I was sweeping," Elise reasoned. But Lily and Thomas were having none of it.

"There were ravens at that other orphanage, and they were here, too!" Lily exclaimed.

"Yeah! That's not just a coincidence. She had to have been involved. I just know it." Thomas nodded firmly.

"Ravenkin saved us all!" Lily cheered. "She's the hero for all the orphans in the whole city!"

"She's so cool. She'll probably be on the news again soon for taking down another corrupt orphanage."

"Yeah! She'll save us all with the help of her ravens!"

"Ravenkin—*Caw!*" Thomas flapped his arms like a bird as he jumped up onto his feet.

Elise and Beth watched with stunned smiles as Lily mirrored him, and then the other kids did much of the same. They all ran around the main living space, cawing like ravens and cheering her given name over and over again until they finally disappeared up the stairs. Beth grinned at her in the quiet that crept in.

"Not a superhero, huh?"

Elise shoved her playfully. "They're just playing around. They're kids."

Beth laughed. "Maybe, but they aren't wrong."

"What do you mean?"

"You saved two orphanages now, Elise. You exposed their horrors to the public, brought awareness to the issues, and saved all these kids from further abuse. You are a superhero."

Elise shrugged. "I just wanted to help them. No one should have to live in the conditions we all have."

"You're right. And that mindset is why you've been successful twice now."

"I guess."

Elise's mind drifted to Lily and Thomas' conversation. They saw her as a savior of orphans, and Orion, earlier on the news, said much of the same. With the help of Beth and the Blackwings, she had taken down two horrific people and exposed their abuse to the public. Beth was right; she had done well. But could she do more?

She'll probably be on the news again soon for taking down another corrupt orphanage. Thomas' words ran through her mind again and again. Was she thinking too small? She had faced the abuse of her own orphanage, and now had seen the abuse spread and worsen at yet another one. Was she being ignorant to the fact that many other orphanages probably consisted of many of the same horrific practices?

Why stop here? she thought. *Why not be the hero that Lily and Thomas looked up to so much?*

"You're thinking." Beth smirked. "Tell me what you're thinking."

Elise shifted on the couch so she could face her friend. "We took down Ravensford with little issue. Do you think...?"

"We could do it again?" Beth finished for her.

Elise gazed at her friend. Normally, she was more soft-spoken. But in this moment, she was confident, her gaze hard and determined. She eyed the TV just as the Ravensford headline rolled along the bottom of the screen yet again.

"What's stopping us?" Beth asked, turning her bright gaze to Elise.

Elise's lips curled into a smile. "Then it's decided. I'll talk to the Blackwings tomorrow."

"Then I guess it's time to find our next target." Beth pushed herself up, and Elise followed.

The two made their way upstairs and settled in the dark bedroom behind Beth's computer. They scouted out the next orphanage to the chorus of cheering kids running up and down the halls outside, yelling "Ravenkin!" again and again.

~

THE FLOOD OF KIDS FROM RAVENSFORD ARRIVED soon after their hit.

Just as Alexa had said on the news, the petitions to shut down Ravensford came swiftly and were firmly embraced by the members of their city. Ravensford's doors were shut and locked within three days of its closing. The children were divided and sent to the surrounding orphanages, along with hefty bonuses from the government to support them all.

And that's how three days after their hit, and after watching him give her a name on the news, Elise stood face-to-face with Orion again.

He stepped through the front door, loaded with bags like some kind of pack mule, and Elise found herself wondering how a boy of his size could even carry so much weight. The heavy, sagging bags looked ready to snap his bones into two. But he set them on the floor slowly and gently before he met Elise's eyes. He smiled.

"We meet again," he said, ignoring all the other younger kids rushing past him to get inside and see their new home.

Elise cleared her throat, shaking herself. "Um, I—I don't know what you're talking about."

Orion chuckled. "It's okay. I won't tell."

Tell? Elise's throat constricted. Did he know *she* was Ravenkin, plastered all over the news for the past three days? Did he know that *she* was the one he had made famous with his nickname for her? Did he *know?*

"You got Ravenkin to come help us after you scouted Ravensford, didn't you?" He continued through her silence.

Elise let out the heaviest sigh of relief.

"Yes, uh, I... connected with her by chance. She did the same thing with our orphanage. That's why we lost our headmaster. And after that... well, she wanted to help other kids, too. I just gave her the idea."

"And scouted for her. Apparently, you did a good job." Orion smiled. Up close, Elise found his eyes even brighter and even more beautiful than before.

"Yeah, uh... thanks." Her cheeks flushed pink, and she could feel his eyes lingering on her. She had to turn away to hide her face. "So," she cleared her throat, "you'll be staying here now."

"Seems like it. Ravensford closed so quickly that we barely had time to pack all of our things before they ushered us out."

"Well, you'll be better off here. Ms. Augustine actually cares about all of us, and even in the week or so that she's been in charge, things have been way better."

"I'm glad to hear it." Orion picked up his bags again, and Elise grabbed a couple to help him.

"I'll show you to your room. You have to share it because we're tight on space, but everyone shares here. You'll get used to it."

Orion beamed at her, warm and welcoming. "No problem with me."

Elise shuffled in front of him, and she led him up the stairs and down the hall. She led him to a room with open bunks and found two other younger boys sitting on the upper bunks already, talking. They gave her a look when she opened the door, but once she introduced Orion, they lit up.

They hadn't had an older boy at the orphanage for as long as she could remember. The oldest boy they ever had was adopted at the age of twelve. Elise was the oldest now, and once she hit thirteen, no one had come in that was older than her. It would be... nice to have another older kid here.

Orion set a few of the bags on one bunk and the rest on the other. He told her those bags were for another boy named Nicholas, who was supposed to show up later that afternoon after his interview with police. Orion had taken his bags, however, and said he'd save them for the boy. Elise nodded and turned to let the three boys get to know each other, but Orion followed her out.

"Hey, um, I don't think I ever caught your name."

Elise stopped in the hall. "It's Elise."

"Elise. I like it," he murmured to himself. Elise's cheeks burned, so she turned her head away again. She needed to get out of here. His gaze burned into her back, and she was all too aware of it.

"Thanks for showing me to my room and everything, Elise. It's um, it's good to see a familiar face after so much change."

Elise nodded, refusing to turn around and hoping he didn't think it was because she didn't care about his words. On the contrary, she couldn't get her cheeks to cool off.

"It's no problem. I'm glad you all are safe again."

Orion's voice lowered. "Me, too. Things were getting really bad at Ravensford. And I—well, it doesn't matter now. Anyway, thank you."

Elise nodded and began taking massive strides down the hallway. "Dinner is at six!" she called out before turning the corner and running down the steps, two at a time. She told Ms. Augustine that she'd be back as she rushed out the front door and made her way to the park.

As the sun shined high in the sky, and the cold nipped at her fingertips, Elise plopped down on her bench at the park. The Blackwings joined her within moments, their wings fluttering and flapping at their entrance.

Averin perched on the bench beside her. He glanced up at her with those yellow eyes of his.

"Is something wrong, Elise?"

She shook her head, her cheeks still red with heat. "I just—it's nothing. Don't worry about it." Elise turned to her friend and cleared her throat, ignoring the flush in her cheeks. "We need to talk."

"About what?"

Elise eyed the others, too. "Beth and I decided on our next target. Are you in?"

Averin and the others nodded and squawked with encouragement. "We're in!"

EIGHT

Elise, Beth, and the Blackwings had three more hits in the following three weeks. First, they exposed Gatewood, then Founder's Row, and two days ago, they finished their streak with Collingsworth Orphanage and Childcare Facility—what a mouthful.

After Ravensford, the next targets came quickly and efficiently as each member of Elise's team settled into their roles. Beth was the planner and drew maps when her and Elise scouted. Elise was the executioner and made sure to expose every crack in the orphanages' façades to the world, all while following up with anonymous tips to the police.

Averin worked through the plans and made them foolproof with Beth. Kani and Kumi worked out attack plans for the headmasters, guards, and any other adults or obstacles they might run into. Vrukum was the instigator and the bringer of chaos. And Dolvek was the muscle, attacking, blocking, and protecting the others when needed.

Their team was solid, and after Ravensford's fall, they were unstoppable. The three orphanages were exposed, their headmasters and authority figures shown to the world as violent, abusive, and manipulative.

Some used the government's money the same way that Mrs. Gallagher had, buying luxury goods and exotic vacations for themselves, while others delighted in the abuse and mental torture of the children. But whether it was for money, fear, or pain—all of the people exposed were power-hungry and abused their positions in childcare.

Ravensford was the only one to close down fully, though the others were all put on temporary holds, much like Elise's orphanage after Mrs. Gallagher was taken away. But without the power-hungry individuals running them, Elise knew the kids were in better hands. The news made sure of it, too. They followed her every move.

Ravenkin was everywhere—in the newspapers, on magazine covers, on TV, and even on social media, which Elise didn't participate in, but she heard the other girls in her classes talking about "the raven girl."

Everywhere—everyone knew of Ravenkin. The mysterious girl who broke into orphanages, exposed their abuse, got these abusive leaders arrested, and saved the forgotten children of the city. She was a superhero! She was magic! She had super powers!

And no matter where she went, her ravens followed. Elise finally started to get used to her other abilities, too. She chatted with some of the other ravens, and even brought a few in to help with bigger jobs. She manipulated the shadows around her and used them to hide herself and her team when things got sticky during hits, or immediately after when the press and the police were quick to come. Everyone wanted a glimpse of her, and everyone wanted to know her identity. Her shadows helped keep her hidden.

At the last hit, at Collingsworth, she finally utilized her weapon-making ability, too. When the headmaster of Collingsworth, a rounded, obtuse man, tried to lock her out of his office, she had to come up with other means to get inside. She used the magic from her palm, letting the energy flow from her hand and join with the shadows around her to create an axe. It glittered dark purple in the light and glowed with surging power. She sliced down on the doorknob with one quick thrust, and the knob fell off with a *ding!*

It rolled across the tile floor, and Elise pushed open the door. She faced the man in the open doorway, her purple axe ebbing and flowing with barely contained energy. The man's eyes widened at the weapon, and his face bleached of all color. Elise smirked.

"You've nowhere else to run. It's time to face the consequences of your actions."

The man sagged to the floor in a heap, and Elise could smell before she saw the dark stain on the front of the man's pants. The police had come within minutes of that moment, and by the time they crashed through the front door and ran back to the office, she was gone.

The headmaster was left trembling, mumbling of a raven girl with a purple axe, and walking out in hand-cuffs, a urine stain covering the entirety of the front of his pants. Elise had howled with laughter at the news report that night with Beth at her side. All the kids thought the headmaster's reaction was laughable, but they weren't there to witness the fall of such an angry, gaudy man.

Orion thought the downfalls of the abusive heads of the city orphanages were just as delightful, which Elise was... happy with. He talked fondly of Ravenkin and smiled every time she was mentioned on the news when they all watched it together in the evenings. He always said that her regular attacks didn't surprise him, as it seemed to for everyone else in the city. He expected her to continue her streak of morality. He knew the downfall of Ravensford wouldn't be the last.

Elise talked about Ravenkin once with him, but even as she admired his own admiration of her, she found it hard to keep eye contact when she knew she was keeping the truth from him.

Except for Ravenkin, they grew closer from the moment he moved in after Ravensford closed. He sat with her, Beth, Lily, and Thomas every night at dinner. He went to get ice cream with them regularly. He sat next to Elise or Beth on the school bus every day. And he frequently hung out with Elise after school at the park.

She hadn't been able to talk to the Blackwings as much because of his presence, but she sensed their eyes watching from a distance. They were there if she needed them, and they were never too far away.

It warmed her one afternoon after school when she ended up at the park, sitting on the cold bench, after wiping away the few snowflakes that had settled there from that morning's flurry. Orion had joined her yet again, but after walking in the cold for more than ten minutes and upon arrival at the park, where he saw a man selling hot chocolate from a food cart on the opposite side of the lawn, he said he'd return shortly and shuffled away. Elise smiled to herself as she watched him hunch in the cold and beeline for the food cart.

A soft fluttering echoed from behind her, and

when she glanced down, Averin and the others perched on the wall opposite her.

"Hello, Elise," Averin said.

She smiled and reached into her backpack. She pulled out a packet of crackers and started handing one to each of them. She laughed as their varying degrees of snacking commenced.

"How are you all today?"

Vrukum was the first to respond after shoveling down his cracker whole. "Good! We were waiting for you. You've been walking slower lately."

"Yeah! And you've been with that *boy!*" Kani squawked.

Elise's cheeks flushed, and she knew Averin caught the reaction.

"Yes, well. He lives at the orphanage now, and he has become a... friend of mine."

"Only a friend?" Kumi teased.

"Only a friend," Elise said flatly. "His name is Orion."

"Is he nice to you?" Kani asked.

"Yes. Very much so. Probably a little too nice. He, um... kind of has a thing for Ravenkin."

Kani and Kumi gasped, their feathers ruffling. Vrukum bobbed his head in excitement, while Dolvek watched and listened quietly.

"He doesn't know of your abilities then," Averin said evenly.

Elise shook her head. "I don't... I didn't know how

to tell him. And I don't know... aren't I supposed to keep it a secret or something? Isn't that what normal superheroes do?"

Kumi chuckled, her voice rough and crackling in Elise's mind. "You told Beth. Why not tell him? You trust him, right?"

"I do! I just... I don't know."

Averin tilted his head at her. "Are you... afraid that his ideas of Ravenkin might not be met if he knows who she really is?"

The other four fell silent. Their eyes flickered between Elise to Averin, and then back again. Elise wanted to laugh it off and wave her hand at Averin's comment. She wanted to say, "No! Of course not!" and give him some lame excuse of her social anxiety and nervousness or something. But—well—

Elise sighed. "I'm just me, okay? I'm Elise Winters, an orphan in the city with no family, no savings, no plans for the future, and nothing to my name. And Ravenkin is—she's a beloved superhero! She saves kids, rights the wrongs of the adoption system, and exposes those who have abused it! And I—" Elise swallowed, all of her fears, all of her doubts sitting on her chest like a weight. "I just don't want him to be disappointed by the face under the mask."

"Elise." Averin grabbed her eyes with his own. The pearly orbs were firm, but gentle. She couldn't look away. "Ravenkin is a part of *you*. You are an orphan, but you are also smart, cunning, loving, and so much more. Elise Winters is Ravenkin, so if he admires the superhero, then there's no way he won't love you, too."

Elise stared at her friend and resisted every urge to grab Averin and pull him into a tight, bear hug. She wasn't used to receiving praise, so it was still mostly foreign to her. But Averin, quiet, watchful, and mindful Averin—was so very good at it. He made her eyes burn with barely held back tears.

She wiped at her nose with her sleeve as she sniffled. "Thank you, Averin. Really. I... I appreciate you all more than you can know."

The Blackwings clucked and cooed around her, expressing their own love back to her. She smiled at all of them, but soon enough, they fluttered off as footsteps approached. Elise looked up to find Orion shuffling back to the bench with two coffee cups in his hands. He handed one to her as he took his spot next to her on the bench.

"One hot chocolate, m'lady. Sorry for the wait. The man running the cart made them fresh for us."

Elise took a sip of the scalding liquid to soothe her nerves, not even caring that the top layer of her tongue tingled with a fresh burn.

"Hey, look!" Orion pointed up at the trees across the path from them. Elise looked up and found the Blackwings perched on the branches, watching. "There are ravens up there. How cool!"

Elise murmured into her cup. "Maybe they're Ravenkin's birds."

"Maybe. That would mean she's around here then, right?"

Elise shrugged. "Maybe."

She expected him to get up and look around. Maybe ignore her altogether in his search for Ravenkin. But he surprised her by staying still. He sipped at his own hot drink and squeezed the cup firmly in his bare fingers. She glanced at him from the corner of her vision, and he caught her lingering gaze. Orion smiled.

"What?"

Elise couldn't help herself. "Aren't you going to like... look for her or something?"

Orion's brow raised. "For her?"

"Ravenkin."

"Why would I do that?"

"Because there are ravens here? And if they're hers, then she could be nearby. Don't you want to meet her and find out who she is?"

Orion surprised her again with a shrug. "They could be her birds, or they could just be wild ravens who happen to be here. But even if they were hers, and she *was* nearby, it wouldn't make a difference."

"Why?"

"Because. I'm not here to meet Ravenkin. I'm here because I want to hang out with you, Elise."

"Me?" Elise straightened, her eyes widening on him. "But... why? What's so special about me?"

Orion laughed, the sound smooth and rich like a lilting cello. "Everything?"

Elise huffed. "You're full of it."

"Hey, I'm not kidding." Orion caught her gaze, but he couldn't seem to hold it. His eyes fell to his lap, where he fiddled with his fingers. "I know I've only known you a short time but... I don't know. I feel like I've always known you. It's easy talking to you, and even easier being your friend. I'm... I'm happy you're in my life now, Elise."

Elise stared at him in silence. What was she supposed to say to something like that? She never had someone say anything like that to her before. Sure, Beth and the others complimented her every once in a while, and she loved them dearly. But this—this was different. A different kind of interest. The fluttering in her gut was different for her.

"I, um... you too," she said lamely.

She looked to her right, where the ravens watched from up in a tree. Averin tilted his head at her, like he disapproved of her terrible response, too. But Elise didn't have the words to tell Orion what she really felt. She couldn't think of anything that would be as meaningful to him as his words to her. Her mind drew a blank.

She glanced at the others in the tree, who all watched silently as a breeze made the tree branches dance.

"Do you remember me from that day?" Elise murmured.

Orion glanced up at her. "That day in Ravensford, right? On the steps."

Elise nodded slowly. "Beth and I ran into you on the stairs when we were trying to make our escape. And then when the headmaster blocked the door, you distracted them so we could make a run for it."

"Yeah, I remember. I got quite the punishment that day."

Elise flinched, remembering the cold dark of the room upstairs. She hoped that he wasn't taken to that godforsaken room.

"Hey," he caught her eyes, "I'd do it again and again if I had to. It got you out that day, and that's all that matters."

But Elise shook her head. "You shouldn't have been punished so severely in the first place. That shouldn't even have been an option for those adults caring for you. It's—it's terrible!"

"You're right. They were abusive and power-hungry over all the children, and it was cruel. But that's all behind us now."

"But it's not over. It'll never be over."

"What do you mean?"

Elise glanced up at the Blackwings and felt Orion's gaze on her. "The kids of Ravensford were saved, but how many more are there? In our city, in our state—in *the world.* It's never-ending. There will always be kids who are abused and beaten down and forgotten because they are alone and defenseless. And this system abuses the power it holds over them. But I—I'm going to change that."

"How?"

In that moment, Elise knew exactly what to say to him. She knew exactly how she would convey her feelings.

"Haven't you ever wondered *why* Beth and I were in Ravensford that day?"

"I've thought about it. Why?"

Elise took a steadying breath. "Beth and I were scouting out Ravensford so we could come up with a plan to take it down from the inside. Once we had that plan in place, we pooled our help."

"Your help...?" Orion followed her gaze to the trees. His breath caught as he found the ravens watching and listening from their perches.

"The ravens helped me take down Ravensford Orphanage. Just as they have with our orphanage, and the others after."

Orion's eyes whipped back to her. "You mean—?"

Elise nodded. "I am Ravenkin. And those—" she pointed at the trees "—are the Blackwings."

Orion's dark eyes burned two holes in her head. He couldn't stop staring. His eyes trailed over her features and along her long, dark hair before they flickered to the birds. "The Blackwings is a group of ravens," he mumbled to himself. "They're your... Blackwings. You're Ravenkin."

Elise smiled shyly, that bubbling, fluttering feeling in her gut making her almost nauseous with anxiety.

"Well? Was it what you expected?"

Orion's wavering eyes settled on her. They softened in the gentle light of the receding sun. His fingers stopped moving on his lap; his tension seemed to ease. He smiled at her.

"Ravenkin turning out to be Elise Winters? Yeah, it's exactly what I expected. Actually, no. It's even better."

Elise's cheeks flushed bright red. "Really?"

"Really."

His smile warmed her from the inside out, and at the sight of it, she was glad that she told him the truth. He hadn't reacted how she expected, but at Averin's words running through her head, she saw how ridiculous her fears were. The Blackwings was right—Orion *was* a good person. He liked being with her, he smiled at her, he brought her hot chocolate, which she had long forgotten in her cold hands. But above all else—he cared about her.

"So... do the ravens have names?"

Elise chuckled, waving down her friends. They swooped down and landed on the wall opposite the bench with only a light fluttering of wings. She pointed to each of them and introduced them to Orion. He nodded at each and smiled as she listed off their names.

"Such interesting names. I like them."

"Is his name based off of the constellation Orion?" Averin asked.

She turned to Orion. "Averin is asking where your name came from."

Orion eyed her. "You can talk to them?"

She nodded. "We understand each other. But I'm the only one who can hear their voices. They echo in my head."

"That's so cool!" Orion's smile grew even wider. Elise couldn't help but imagine a child smiling wider as their curiosity piqued. He looked like a kid in a candy store.

"Oh! But yes, to answer your question, Averin—my name is based off of the constellation, Orion. Apparently, my birth parents had a thing for astronomy, but not for supporting the child they mistakenly had."

Elise stifled at his dark joke. She had made many of her own over the years in the same fashion, having known very little about her birth parents. But hearing Orion so casually talk of his own birth parents surprised her.

"Do you know who your birth parents are?" Elise asked gently.

Orion shrugged. "I know their names, and I've looked them up before on the computer at the library. I emailed them once, but I've never met them face-to-face. Nor would I like to."

"You *talked* to them?"

"Yeah. That's how I found out how I got my name. Apparently, my father had just gotten a new telescope, and they were using it on a clear night to see the stars. They started listing constellations and took turns finding them in the sky through the telescope. Orion was the first one they found, and the one they always came back to. And uh, after a night of stargazing, I was conceived and later given the name Orion in remembrance of that night."

"Then Orion was a personal name, something meaningful to them," Elise reasoned. Orion bobbed his head in a wavering nod. "If it meant something to them, and they put the thought behind it, then why didn't they—?"

"Keep me?" Orion finished for her. Elise swallowed past the lump in her throat, but Orion huffed out a dark chuckle. "It's fine. You can say it. We're all in the same boat, after all.

"From what my father told me, I was a mistake. They were young, my father was soon departing for the other side of the world with his military job, my mother was living at home and barely scraping by with money as she finished her education. Neither of them had time, money, or could support a child. So, they made the decision early on to give me up after I was born."

Elise listened in silence. Every orphan in the city had a similar story of being given up or dropped off or forfeited to the state. But rarely did the orphans get to hear the tale of their parents' decision from the source itself. Elise could hardly believe it.

"That's... terrible. I'm so sorry."

Orion waved her off. "It's no big deal. They were kids. They made a mistake, and I'm over it now."

"But their recklessness put you in your situation to begin with. Aren't you at least a little mad?"

Orion's smile tightened a fraction. "I was. At one point after hearing the story, I couldn't stand to even think of them. They were dumb, they made a mistake, and instead of avoiding the mistake altogether or just, I don't know, aborting me—they decided to have me anyway, knowing that they didn't want me." Orion huffed out another heavy, joyless chuckle, but then his shoulders slumped. "I hated them. I hated that because of their foolishness, I was the one who had to suffer, and they didn't even seem to care. They moved on, got married, had kids when they were finally ready, and bought an old ranch in the south. And I—I was stuck in an abusive, horrible, terrible orphanage in the heart of a city that doesn't care about me."

Before she could think, Elise grabbed Orion's hand. She squeezed it gently, letting him know that she was there. He grinned softly and squeezed her hand right back.

"But you know? I'm not angry anymore. Because while this isn't the life I would've asked for, it's what I've been given, and there's no changing that now. And besides, my life... isn't so bad anymore. It's finally looking up."

Elise's cheeks warmed, and Orion squeezed her hand again, his smile, thorny and cold, softening again to something warm and gentle. She found herself thinking that she never wanted to see that cold smile on his lips again. She would do anything—anything—to keep him happy and smiling and carefree.

"You're part of a new family now. Ours," Elise said, her voice unusually tender.

"Yeah? You'll have me?"

"It isn't perfect, and it's an odd bunch of orphans, ravens, and a bit of justice, but we would be happy to have you."

Orion's dark eyes burned bright in the waning light. Elise couldn't look away as her chest simmered with a warm, flickering fire. She had put herself out there, more than ever before. And she found herself hoping that Orion wouldn't turn away.

He grinned instead. "I will graciously accept your offer. But I do have one condition."

Elise raised a brow. "What is that?"

"I want to help you take down the heads of corrupt orphanages."

Elise stared at him. He hadn't said he wanted to help Ravenkin. He wanted to help *her*. After hearing the story of his birth parents, after seeing the bruises and the scars on his body from his time at Ravensford, and now—seeing the burning fire in his dark eyes, she knew she had already made a decision.

"Okay," she said.

"Really?"

"Really."

The ravens squawked and cooed their cheers from the wall. Elise and Orion laughed as the sun finally dipped below the horizon. They said their goodbyes to the birds, and Elise promised to come see them again tomorrow. With that, her and Orion made their way back to the orphanage, and as they walked side-by-side on the sidewalk, Elise felt the warmth of his skin melt the cold in her fingers. She never did let go of his hand.

She peeked up at him as they walked under a streetlight and found him peeking right back at her. Her cheeks burned, but he smiled. He squeezed her hand again.

CHAPTER

NINE

Oнce Oʀion joined the group, the roles shifted.

Beth handled the preemptive research and took on the task of making anonymous tips to the government, police, and the news agencies in the area before a hit. Orion was the charmer and the map artist, and went with Elise to scout the orphanages beforehand. He got them in and out of the buildings with ease, and if someone questioned them, he handled all the interactions seamlessly. That left Elise and the ravens. When the plan was made and the time came, they brought the corrupt organizations down from the inside.

They hit one orphanage after another when they each got a handle on their roles. They worked to each other's strengths, and the process became much quicker, more reliable, and more efficient. They went from deciding on a target and doing a hit within a week to doing it in mere days. Elise could move swiftly under this rhythm, and all of them cheered in victory as power-hungry and abusive headmasters were taken down one by one.

They showed the world the horrors that they inflicted upon children, and made the city face the children they had so eagerly forgotten about and brushed aside.

The news grew hungrier each day for stories of Ravenkin. They wanted to know her whereabouts; they wanted to track her next move and contemplated where she would hit next.

This threat should make the corrupt headmasters running these orphanages think twice about what they were doing. But they were cocky, and the thought of a girl who could talk to ravens seemed too crazy to be real.

There would *always* be more corruption to take down. Elise, furious with each and every one of their targets, wouldn't stop until the corruption was gone.

In the following weeks, everyone in the city was on their toes, waiting for her next move, and eager for a glance of the girl who could talk to ravens and wield shadow weapons. More and more witnesses emerged, who claimed to have seen her during or after a hit. They talked of her ability to communicate with the ravens, yes, but they also did her bidding. They weren't wild birds pecking and clawing at headmasters. They were smart, calculated, and worked alongside Ravenkin as partners.

In addition to the ravens, however, there were a growing number of reports on her wielding shadows. The most common instance was her shadow weapon wielding. One man claimed to have seen her holding a giant chain with an axe on one end and a spiked ball on the other. What could she say? It was efficient and had a weapon on both sides, to be used for whatever she needed. It was her weapon of choice.

A common theme with all of these reports lingered. The headline raced across the screen or spread across the cover of some magazine or newspaper nearly every day.

Who was Ravenkin?

Who was she? Was she an orphan, too? Was she a victim of abuse and corruption in the system? Is that why she targeted orphanages? Where was she from? What was her age? Who—? What—? *Why—?*

No one knew. She swooped in for a hit, and with the help of her ravens and weapons, she brought the headmasters to their knees, and just when the authorities and news vans showed up—she disappeared. Ravenkin was a ghost, one who was quickly admired by the city and all of its children.

Elise stared at the kids passing by on the sidewalk as she strolled through the park with Orion and Beth. Kids who had ravens on their shirts, who had masks with raven beaks on the front, who ran beside their parents, pushing a stroller, flapping their arms like a flying bird, and swooping down to fight crime.

Orion and Beth muffled their laughs as Elise watched wide-eyed. It was like... she was some kind superhero. Just as Beth had said.

Along with her own reputation growing, Elise's Blackwings had grown, too. Flocks from all across the city flew in to help her and Averin in their quest to expose the wrongdoings of the system and make things right for the kids suffering from it.

At first, she had been hesitant to reach out to other the ravens, even if her power allowed her to talk to any and all of them. Even though she could, she didn't know if she should. The Blackwings *chose* her. They wanted her to be part of their family and part of their team. But the other groups of ravens... would they accept her, too?

It turned out that they did. They were inspired by her story and wanted to help her succeed, too. So, she created a network of ravens from one end of the city to the other. The ravens watched and listened, and then reported their findings to the next, and then they sent the information to the next, and the next, and the next, until it got back to her. She got reports from every direction, about child abuse, about new targets, about the news vans and government agencies involved with Ravenkin's deeds. They kept an eye on everything going on in the city so she could be prepared, so she could decide on future hits, so she could continue to do what was right.

But Elise wanted something bigger. Something better. After ten—twenty—hits on small orphanages, she was ready to take on a larger issue. She wanted to strike the heart of the city and have everyone who was watching pause—think—and adjust. She wanted to ignite that fear that if someone hurt a child—Ravenkin would strike them down.

So, Elise looked beyond the small targets and moved closer to the heart of the city. There, she found it. There, she decided on her next target. The biggest, the baddest, and one of the most funded orphanages in the city—

Havensworth.

Elise sat in her bedroom that evening after a day of snooping around the outside of Havensworth with Orion. Beth, Orion, and the ravens all huddled around her in the small room, the window cracked open, and the door locked to prevent intruding ears.

"I don't know, Elise. Havensworth is huge." Beth hesitated.

"That's why we need to bring it down, Beth!" Elise raised her voice. "Don't you see? All we've done so far has led us to this moment. We're prepared, and we're ready."

"You've prepared to take on smaller orphanages, and you do that well. But Havensworth—it's *gigantic*, and it's funded more by the state and city government."

"So?"

"*So*—it'll have more resources, more guards and protection, and more adults to bypass."

"We didn't see many when we went there today," Elise countered.

Beth looked to Orion, her eyes pleading for some sense.

Orion shrugged. "We only stayed on the outside today, but I didn't see more than two enter and exit the building."

"Exactly!" Elise glanced over her shoulder at the birds. "And you guys? Did you see any more adults around the building?"

Averin shook his head. "We counted two in and out the front door, and one who left through the back to take out trash to the dumpster."

"None of them were guards or uniformed," Kumi noted, too.

"See? We'll be fine, Beth!" Elise exclaimed.

"You say that, but you have no way of knowing. Plus, the whole city is watching you now. Ravenkin has more eyes on her than ever before. If one thing goes wrong, it could put you in an unsafe situation, *and* the whole city will know about it." Beth waved her hands in the air to enunciate her point.

"You're being paranoid. I have the ravens to support me, and if I need them, the rest of the ravens in the entire city. They will come to our aid."

"They've helped relay messages to you, but they haven't taken part in a hit yet," Beth pointed out.

"So? Why does that matter? They'd help if I asked them to," Elise said sharply.

"But they're only *birds*, Elise!"

The room fell silent. Elise's eyes hardened into dark, glowing orbs. Beth winced under her friend's gaze, but she did not back down.

"What do you mean by that?" Elise murmured, her voice low and dangerous.

"I mean, no offense, truly, Averin—" Beth met the stern gaze of Averin and glanced across the others behind him. "I appreciate all that you guys have done for us and for Elise. But if something bad happens, if the headmaster or the guards or the adults at Havensworth are ready for you and do something big to hurt any one of you—is it really worth it? You won't be able to escape on your own."

Averin's eyes flicked to Elise while the other birds glanced back and forth between the girls.

"She may have a point, Elise," Averin said evenly. Always so calm, always so even and collected. Elise gritted her teeth.

"She doesn't! We can *do this*, Averin. We've done it countless times before, and we can do it again. Don't you trust me?"

Averin tilted his head. "Of course, we do. But we also don't want to see you hurt. Or potentially get hurt ourselves."

"You won't."

Averin eyed the other birds, waiting for their responses. Kani chimed in first, always the eager one.

"I will always be in. I want to take down some serious corrupt butts." She snickered.

Kumi followed her twin. "If Elise is certain of our safety, then I'm in, too."

"Hell, yeah, I'm in!" Vrukum squawked.

Dolvek watched them all quietly before he too nodded. "I will take part, too."

Averin turned his gaze to Elise. "We trust you, Elise. If you think this is possible, and the safety of the Blackwings is assured, then we are in."

Elise grinned. "Good. The ravens are in then. Orion?"

She turned her gaze to the boy at her side. He scratched the back of his neck.

"It *is* huge, Elise." He wavered. She opened her mouth to argue, but he started again. "But if you think it's possible, then I will follow you. Besides, somebody has to make sure you get in and out safely."

That soft, curling smile of his warmed her chest. She nudged his shoulder gently and couldn't hide the smile herself. But then she turned to face the final person in the room. Beth sat on her bunk, legs crossed, and her shoulders hunched with tension. Elise tried to assuage her with a softer gaze. She leaned forward and whispered, low and gently, to Beth.

"Beth, please. You're the brains behind the operation. We need you."

Beth's thin lips curled into a pinched frown. "You could get hurt, Elise."

"I won't, okay?"

Beth stared at her, and Elise forced her own lips into a lilting smile. She nudged Beth's leg with her hand. "Come on, I'll be okay."

"Promise?"

Elise nodded once. "I promise."

Beth sighed. "Fine."

Elise nearly smacked her head on the above bed as she jumped up from her bunk in a victory cheer. Beth and Orion chuckled as she did a little victory dance in the center of the small bedroom. The ravens squawked their own laughs, and Kani, Kumi, and Vrukum danced themselves.

After a short round of dancing and jokes, all of them settled in. Beth cracked her laptop open, and they started making a plan to expose Havensworth. It'll be their biggest hit yet, and they weren't about to slip up on their planning.

Beth pulled up the orphanage's website and jotted down bullet point after bullet point of information. She noted that there had been a map of the building and all its amenities at one point, but the heads running the website had taken it down.

"Probably because they're afraid Ravenkin would use it against them," Elise said.

Beth nodded, that pinch she had on her lips while she worked was still very much intact. "Probably."

"It's fine. We'll just gather all the information we can and go there to map out the building, just as we have before," Orion said easily.

Elise nodded before turning to the birds. "And you guys, can you relay the new target to the other ravens? They can be lookouts for us, and if we need backup, they should be prepared."

Averin nodded while the others bobbed their heads, too. One by one, they hopped out the window and flew off, Averin standing on the window ledge last. He gave Elise one final look.

"This will work, won't it?"

Elise smiled. "It'll work. We'll be okay. Trust me."

Averin nodded and flew off to the others, leaving the rest of them to sit huddled in the small room for the rest of the afternoon. They spent all day creating a solid plan, writing down the numbers of the local government agency and the news stations, writing down times, places, meeting points... and once the sun had dropped and their bellies gurgled for food, they all left the stuffy room, made their way down into the kitchen, and Orion and Elise threw together grilled cheese sandwiches and tomato soup.

The three of them sat together at the kitchen counter, munching on their sandwiches and soaking in the heat they provided. They joined the younger kids in front of the TV afterward and settled in to watch cartoons with them. Lily snuggled up to Elise's side while Thomas sat like a pretzel by her feet. Beth sat nearby, and Orion sat on her other side. Elise smiled at them all as the high-pitched voices of the cartoon characters whined through the screen.

This was her family. This was the group she wanted to protect. And she wanted the rest of the city's orphans to feel the same way about each other. They deserved to feel safe, to feel loved and cared for. Her attack on Havensworth would do just that. She scooted closer to Orion. He smiled down at her, all traces of bruising, scratches, and cuts gone. He had finally started to gain some weight and fill into his tall, lean figure. She helped give him a safe space to heal. She would do that for every other orphaned child in the city, too.

But she could think about Havensworth more tomorrow. For now, she pulled a snoozing Lily tighter into her side and let Orion's fingers interlace themselves through her own. Tonight, she would be happy and safe.

Tonight, she would just be Elise Winters.

CHAPTER

TEN

ELISE, ORION, BETH, AND THE RAVENS FLOCKED TO Havensworth three days later.

Their plan had been set, as smooth and as seamless as every other hit. They had a map, they knew exactly where to go and when, and once Elise entered with the birds, Beth would notify the police, and Orion would call forth the storm of media. They all settled on the sidewalks across the street from the towering building.

The sign out front with the orphanage's name, scrawled loopy and elegant, glared at them. Elise spat on the sidewalk.

"Ready to go?" Orion gave her a quick once-over.

Elise bounced on her heels. She itched to begin. "Yes, I'm ready. I've been ready."

Beth gave her friend a quick glance, and Elise could see the worry and uncertainty lingering there. She let out a sigh.

"Beth, I'll be fine. We went over this, and we have our plan. It's airtight."

"I know, I just... worry."

"Well, try not to, okay? We'll be fine, and everything will go smoothly, just as before. In and out, right?"

"In and out. And you leave immediately if anything differs from our plan. Got it?"

Elise nodded begrudgingly. "Got it."

It was Beth's turn to let out a shuddering sigh. She pulled Elise into a hug, something the girls weren't accustomed to. Elise was rigid at first, but feeling Beth's anxiety and worry creep into her, she softened. She wrapped her arms around her friend and squeezed tight.

"Fifteen minutes. That's it. And then this will all be over," Elise whispered into her friend's hair.

Beth nodded. "Just be careful, okay?"

"I will. Promise."

Elise pulled away from her friend, and both of

them avoided eye contact as they straightened them-selves again. Orion smiled at her once, and that was all the reassurance she needed. Elise turned toward the towering behemoth of a building and stepped across the street. She didn't have to check over her shoulder to know that the Blackwings followed.

They stayed close, poised and ready to aid her. Elise stopped at the front door, and with one more nod at her friends and a look at Averin, she pulled down her mask. She had started wearing one after Ravens-ford due to the wide press coverage of Ravenkin. She wanted to keep doing what she was doing, but she didn't need the whole city knowing her identity. Like her ravens, the mask protected her.

Once it was comfortably in place, she turned the handle and stepped inside.

Havensworth was quieter than it had been days ago when Elise and Orion came through to scout the building and draw their map. Where kids had once been bustling around, adults herding them to corners and rooms to quiet down, and the thin, lanky head-master standing outside his office, yelling at a child for leaving crumbs on his plate after lunch—the main living room was silent now.

Where were all the kids? The place looked like it had been abandoned.

Elise stepped forward cautiously, each footfall making the wooden floorboards creak under her weight. She held her breath as she crept toward the headmaster's office, the only sounds being the ticking clock on the wall above the office, and the slight fluttering of wings behind and above her as the ravens settled into their positions. Elise stopped outside the office and reached for the door handle, but as she squeezed the cold metal in her hand, she sensed that something was off. She pushed open the door and flinched as the hinges creaked when it opened.

Elise had the pulsing stone in her hand at the ready. It glowed and flickered as the shadows lingered around her palm, eager to be shaped into a weapon. She tightened her fist and called forth the shadows as the door swung open the rest of the way. But her hands dropped when the office was also empty.

What was going on? Where was everyone?

Maybe they all went on some kind of trip today, she thought.

It would be just her luck to plan a hit on a day when no one was there. She sighed and turned back toward the exit. The birds came swooping down to meet her in the empty space.

"Where is everyone?" Kani mirrored her own thoughts aloud.

Elise shrugged. "I have no idea."

Vrukum sighed. "What a waste."

"But it's not only the kids. The adults, the headmaster... *everyone* is gone." Averin glanced around.

"Maybe they went on a trip or something?" Kumi suggested.

Elise shook her head. Goosebumps rising on her arms as they all stood there out in the open, silent room. "We never went on trips at our orphanage. Mrs. Gallagher wasn't even willing to buy us books for school, much less a trip for pure enjoyment. No, something's off. I just—"

Elise didn't have time to finish her sentence before the ravens were scooped up in fishing nets and hauled away at the headmaster's hands.

"No!" she cried out, the birds squawking and screeching as they fought against the fabric.

The spindly headmaster grinned at her, his crooked teeth yellow matching his wicked smile. He held the opening to the fishing net closed in his tight, boney fist. He yanked the net up in the air and let the birds fumble as they fell over themselves, caught and tangled in the net. They cried out in protest, but one ear-piercing screech in particular made her blood freeze.

Averin looked at her through the net, his pearly eyes narrowed in pain as his wing curled behind him at an odd, unnatural angle.

"Stop!" Elise shrieked, rushing toward the man. The shadows in her palm flared, and her weapon of choice started to appear. "You're hurting them!"

But he held up something that stopped her in her tracks. The light streaming in from the windows glimmered and reflected off the dark metal. He pointed the gun at the Blackwings and cocked it back.

"Take one more step, and I will kill them." The man's voice was as ragged as his appearance. How could someone so frail and weak be so menacing? He grinned as her weapon dissipated, and she held up both hands.

"Good, we understand each other then. Now, who are you?" he asked.

Elise stared at him through the holes in her mask. Her fingers shook with a mixture of fear, anger, and barely contained rage. She couldn't make her tongue move even if she wanted to.

"Show yourself!" the man yelled, his crackling voice filling the sea of silence around them.

Elise flinched at his volume, but she refused to pull down her mask. "Who I am is not important."

"Ha! It sure as hell is. And whether or not you tell me will be irrelevant when the cops get here to arrest you."

"Arrest *me*?" Elise sputtered.

"Yes, you! You're trespassing, you've come with the intent to harass me, and potentially batter me." He chuckled, his laugh dark and throaty. "You think you can throw on a mask and be a *hero* in the city, and expect everyone to thank you. But you're not a hero. You're a vigilante, and no matter what the media says and what names they give you, the police want you captured."

The shaking in Elise's fingers spread through her

arms, and then the rest of her. He was lying. This man —this disgusting, *filth*—was lying to her.

"I'm not the criminal here." She spat. "I have been saving abused and mistreated children. *You* are the problem here. *You* are the one causing so much pain and abuse. And for what? A little bit of money, power, control?"

The man shook his head with a chuckle. "You're only a child yourself. You don't understand."

"I understand that you're a power-hungry man who has no control over his own life, so to make up for it, you abuse your control over small, innocent children who can do nothing to protect themselves. You hurt them, you lie to them, you mistreat them, and then when they fail or slip up, you blame it all on them." Elise was so furious that her eyes began to tear up. "People like you tear down the kids you're supposed to love and support. You make us feel like dirt—worthless and unlovable. You make us feel like we're not even human beings! We're nothing, and we'll never be anything. That's what people like you do. That's how people like you make *us* feel. But that's wrong, and everything you've said to tear us down every day of our lives is wrong."

Elise's fury warped and burned bright in her chest. Everything she had felt, everything she had lived through, everything she had suffered—fueled her in the here and now. And this crooked, wicked little man would *not* make her believe that she was the villain.

"Each and every child is worthy, and each and every one of us has potential," she continued. "We all just want to live happily. We all want to be loved, to be cared for, to thrive. But people like *you* suffocate us all so you can put another dollar from the government into your pocket."

The man chuckled yet again, and Elise's rage flared.

"You're mistaken, my dear, and clearly, you think just like all of the other children. You will never understand the pressures of running an orphanage. Of keeping funding intact, of supporting hundreds of kids at a time, many of whom are unappreciative and unwilling to work with us, either. It isn't as easy as you think, and most of the time, if you are punished, you deserved it."

Elise's mind flashed back to all the times when Mrs. Gallagher had taken it upon herself to punish Elise for missing the bus, missing one dust bunny while sweeping, talking too loudly, *laughing* too loudly, wearing clothes that looked too "homeless," and attempting to read for a class she claimed was worthless and that Elise had no future in.

Elise gritted her teeth. She didn't deserve any of those punishments, and she refused to be made to feel guilty about them. She was a child! She had the right to live and thrive in her own life.

"No, sir. These kids—they have *never* deserved the life you have given them." Elise ground out, her throat constricting. "Even if times are difficult, and your support is lacking, there is no reason at all for you to take out your frustrations on innocent, defenseless children. They are all alone in the world, orphaned and abandoned. You should be showing them love, support, and kindness so they can grow into the best person they can be, and hopefully, get adopted into a new family. But you don't. You bury them. You degrade them, you make them feel guilty for their dreams and desires, and you make them feel small and worthless. You make sure they can't do anything on their own, and then you keep them here so you can continue to receive money that you then use for yourself."

Elise glared at the man. The ravens had fallen quiet as her voice rose louder and louder. She quaked in her spot, remembering Mrs. Gallagher's cruel smirk, her lilting laugh, her self-righteous attitude. She never cared about the children she was tasked to watch over. They were a means for profit; that's it. And this man before her was no different.

The headmaster's gaze darkened, but that crooked smirk of his didn't disappear.

"You're a joke, child. Pretend all you want, but know that it's only *pretend*."

The magic ebbed and flowed in Elise's palm, begging to be let out, to be wielded. She squeezed her fingers into a tight fist. She couldn't. She couldn't risk using her magic with that gun pointed at her friends.

"Release them," she said flatly. "Let my friends go. They have nothing to do with this."

The man hawked out a laugh. "I've heard all about you, *Ravenkin*. I'm not stupid. I know what you and your ravens do together."

"Let them go," Elise repeated, her jaw cracking and popping under pressure.

The man's eyes traveled up and down her body. "You're a child in a mask, pretending to be a hero. You're friends with *birds*, and somehow, you think that will make a difference." He huffed out a harsh chuckle. "You're a freak."

A freak.

"You're a freak!" Brittney had called her. Just as her friends fired spitballs at her, tore her books apart, copied her tests, got her in trouble, and then attacked her in the park as she cried out for help.

"You're a freak." Distant sirens wailed outside the four walls of the building. The police were coming, and the press would be soon to follow. This was it. This was all going to come to an end, here and now.

"You're a freak." Elise took one last look at the Blackwings, a mess of wings and feathers all clumped together uncomfortably in that net. They looked at her with worried, sad eyes. They had stopped her bullies that day in the park, and then they asked her to be part of their family. They had saved her that day. And now, no matter what happened—she would do the same.

"Sounds like the cops are almost here." He

laughed, squeezing the net tighter. "I guess you had a good run. But you're weak, even with your birds. That was the key to your inevitable downfall."

He's right, she thought. She wasn't strong. Physically, she never really had been. But she wasn't weak. Because while she wasn't strong on her own, she had her family, she had her friends, and she had the strength of the Blackwings. They had shown her love, support, and kindness, and with that, she could do anything.

Elise closed her eyes and focused all of her energy on the marble in her hand. The magic glowed and swirled there, eager and ready to be used. She pooled the magic she had, letting it burn brighter and grow stronger as it raced through her. It tingled and itched in her veins, burning to be wielded as the living thing it was. Elise gritted her teeth as the headmaster asked what she was doing. But she ignored him. She had to focus—she had to, here and now.

She molded the racing shadows into the fine, sharp edge of a knife inside her. She took a deep, steadying breath, and she opened her eyes. She met Averin's eyes and found his gaze wide with worry. Not for himself, she knew. But for her—for the Blackwings.

It's okay, she thought to him, *this isn't the end.*

The marble burned in her skin, and Elise's hand shook as she tried to harness the raging magic within her.

Help! She called out into the void. *Please, we need help!*

The marble boiled with heat and energy. Elise threw her hands into the air in a wide V, and the bright flash of energy filled the room with a blinding glow. The burning in her hand ceased, the magic pulsing within her settled and dissipated, and as the bright flash faded and her eyes adjusted, she found the headmaster blinking at her in confusion. He looked around the room, and when he found nothing amiss, that wicked smile crept back onto his lips.

"Looks like you failed. Again." He snickered.

The blaring sirens grew so close outside that she imagined the cops were right outside the building. The press would be here now, following the activity of the police and Beth's call. The surrounding citizens of the city probably lingered outside with all the commotion. They all assumed Ravenkin had taken down another headmaster and exposed the biggest orphanage in the city. That was the plan.

But the plan—had failed.

Elise dropped her arms and hung her head. She couldn't meet Averin's burning gaze as the embarrassment, the guilt, the despair started to trickle in. She had failed. Not only to bring down Havensworth, but she had failed her friends. She had gotten the Blackwings caught and now—now they would probably be—

Her eyes flew up to Averin's, wide and burning with unshed tears. But Averin's weren't harsh or accusing. He looked at her with a softness she couldn't stand. After everything, after all her assurances, all her planning, all her promises—she had gotten them hurt. And still, he looked at her with a gentle kindness.

"It's okay," he said softly. "We'll be okay."

Elise's eyes burned, and a scream rose up in her throat. This couldn't be it. Her magic couldn't have failed her. Not after everything she had done. Not after everything she had accomplished. Her legs wobbled, threatening to crumble underneath her. The sirens stopped; car doors slammed outside. The cops were here, and they were preparing to crash in. Elise let out a slow, ragged breath.

This was it. This was the end to Ravenkin, and the end to the Blackwings.

But then everything went still. All of the sounds outside went silent, and the blanketing quiet inside seemed to expand. Elise heard ringing in her head as the silence crept in. She paused her racing thoughts. She focused, and there, she heard it.

It started as a low rumble, like the sound of a far-off thunderstorm. But then, the rumble grew louder, closer, more violent. At first, Elise thought it might have been an earthquake, but then she heard the blaring squawks echoing outside. Her chest tightened as a shred of hopefulness snuck its way into her heart.

The rumble grew and expanded into a deep roar of screeches and flapping wings. She looked up above her and found the skylights in the ceiling blacked out with feathers racing by. They surrounded the building. She couldn't know how many of them were outside, but she could sense their presence.

The ravens—the ones she and Averin had connected with—she called upon them, and they came. Her ravens came to help.

Elise's cheeks cracked with the wide smile on her lips. She laughed as the black shadow of fluttering wings and throaty screeches circled the building in a storm. They came! They actually came! The headmaster glanced at the multiple windows around them, but those were also blotted out by black feathers. Sweat beaded on his brow as he clenched the metal of the gun tighter in his fist.

Elise stepped toward the front door and stopped with one hand on the handle.

"Wait! Stop!" the headmaster called out.

Elise smirked to herself. "What? They're just *birds*."

She cracked the door open on squeaking hinges, and the room was instantly filled with shrill *caws* from outside. Elise thought a hundred birds might show up, but she never imagined to see the hundreds—no thousands!—of birds that flew around the building, perched on every surface, lined the sidewalks, guarded the doors and windows, and watched from the trees across the street. It was like a windstorm of ravens, and Elise couldn't stop her smirk.

She turned her dark gaze to the headmaster, who

stood hunched and trembling in his spot. His gun looked to be all but forgotten, hanging limply in his boney hand. He looked like he was ready to run, or perhaps, stain his pants. She pointed a lean finger at him.

"Let them go, or I will tell all of my friends here to attack."

The man hesitated, his hand shaking around the net. He glanced behind her out the open door, but it wasn't the threat of the cops or his inevitable arrest that worried him. It was the storm of ravens, waiting for their command.

Elise raised a brow at him. "Well? What will it be?"

The headmaster took one more look before he dropped the sack of net onto the floor and bolted. Elise didn't bother chasing him as he ran for the back door. He wouldn't get far. And he didn't, she judged by the sound of ensuing shrieks and wings flapping. But soon, the fluttering wings stopped, and in its place, she heard a voice cry out.

"Stop! Hands up!"

That's when she knew it was over. Havensworth would be safe again, and that awful man would be removed from his position. But Elise didn't care about that. She didn't care about anything else but the Blackwings. She raced for the bundle of net on the floor and quickly made work of smoothing it out. She helped the ravens escape the binds of the net, detangling wings and talons as she went. It was when she got to Averin that the tears started to flow.

"I'm so sorry, Averin. I didn't mean for this to happen. I just—I'm so sorry." She rushed out as she worked on detangling his twisted wing. She used slow and gentle fingers to pull the fabric away as Averin held in his flinches like a trooper.

"Stop apologizing, Elise. We signed up for this, and we agreed to help. It was part of the risk. It isn't your fault."

"It is! Just look at what happened, and your poor wing—"

"My wing will heal. And now, because of what you did here today, the children at Havensworth will heal, too."

He looked up at her with those gentle, pearly eyes, and Elise sniffled. After her argument with the headmaster, she didn't realize how much she needed to hear these words. She unwound the last bit of net around Averin's wing and pulled it gently back to his side. Averin moved it slowly at first, testing it, but then he couldn't hide his flinch.

Elise held out her hands. Averin looked at them in question.

"Come on. You can't fly out of here, so I'll carry you."

Averin looked to his friends, who watched in sullen silence. But then he sighed and let her scoop him up. She set him on her shoulder, and Averin perched there steadily, easing up on his talons so they didn't stab into her shoulder. She told the others that they should go.

"We're not leaving you behind to defend yourself!" Kumi screeched.

"Yeah! Who knows what the cops will do if that crazy man was right?" Kani agreed.

Elise shook her head. "It doesn't matter what they do to me. They can't do much, anyway. I'm a minor, and the only real crime I've committed is trespassing. Which the headmasters would have to press charges on, and they're all currently either in jail or being investigated."

The birds all wavered, a sea of bobbing heads and shrugs. Elise chuckled at them.

"I'll be fine, okay? You all need to get away from here, though. I don't want to take any chances and have something happen to you all. And Averin," she patted his foot, "will come with me. I'll get him fixed up and back to you all later."

The ravens looked back and forth between each other, Elise, and Averin. The girl and Averin were their leaders, after all. They were directionless.

"Go," Averin said evenly. "We will meet up later in the park, at our regular spot."

The ravens nodded and flew out the door once Elise reopened it. Elise paused in the shadow of the doorway. There were ravens, cops, cameras, and civilians on every spot of the sidewalk and road in front of the building. They were all clawing to get a closer look, to see the girl who had been proclaimed a hero and called forth a storm of ravens to her aid. She took a sharp intake of breath.

"Hey," Averin squeezed her shoulder gently, "it will be okay. You can do this."

"I don't know," Elise murmured. "All eyes are on me. I kind of wish I could just disappear in the shadows again."

"You can't run any longer, Elise. It's time."

Elise glanced over the eager crowd of people and spotted her friends on the sidewalk across the street, right where she had left them before this debacle. Orion and Beth looked toward her with worried, tense gazes. She had been longer than twenty minutes. She had called forth all the ravens in the city. And her plan had failed.

But—she was safe. The Blackwings were safe and mostly unharmed. And the children of Havensworth would be safe from here on out. Averin was right; she couldn't run from this.

It was time.

She stepped out into the sunshine on an unusually warm winter day, the first sign of the cold season coming to an end, and the warmth and new beginnings of Spring taking over. Cameras flashed, and cops tensed all around her. She stopped on the stoop of the building, Averin perched on her shoulder, and she lifted her hands to the air.

Thank you for all your help. Thank you, she thought.

She sent her thanks into the air with a burst of her magic, and within moments, the ravens started to flap their wings to clear out. They were a shrill chorus of squawks and calls to one another, almost a victory screech of sorts. Elise smiled up at them, basking in the sea of black feathers and kinship. Once most of the sea had thinned, she lowered her hands and faced the crowd before her.

Averin stood straight on her shoulder, and she sensed the other four of the Blackwings perched behind her above the doorway to the orphanage. Cameras flashed, and she could see the pictures on the papers tomorrow already. But she didn't care about her publicity, and she didn't care about her reputation. The children of Havensworth were safe now, and her family was safe, too.

Elise let out a breath she hadn't realized she'd been holding. Then she stepped into the crowd to join her friends.

CHAPTER

ELEVEN

the park and asked the man running it for two ice cream cones. Her purple floral sundress shimmied around her knees as she swung the loose fabric in circles around her while she waited.

It was finally warm enough to wear dresses and shorts in the city. The buildings did a good job of providing cool shade in the summertime, but in the

Spring, they prevented that soft, warm light from reaching everyone. That's why Elise spent most of her time at the park, where the buildings hung back, the trees sprouted with new blossoms, the grass grew greener and higher every day, and the sun could kiss her tanned skin.

The man handed her the cones and an extra baggie of broken cone pieces, just as she always asked for. She smiled her thanks and handed him some bills, telling him to keep the change. She dangled the baggie of cone pieces on one finger and carried the two cones with the rest as she made her way back along the sidewalk to her favorite bench. She licked at the chocolate ice cream in one cone and licked her lips clean. Chocolate had always been her favorite.

As she approached, two young boys, probably in middle school, sat on another bench and huddled together as they peered at one of their phones. She heard them giggle. The reporter's voice rang out loudly from the phone's speaker.

"After a monumental display of her abilities at Havensworth Orphanage, the streets were covered with ravens. People all over the city have started to notice and respect these birds that are normally noted as mischievous and misfortune. But Ravenkin has changed the people's ideals on these birds. She has shown their strength and power in numbers, and has created quite the fearsome image. But the question still stands: who is Ravenkin?"

After the debacle at Havensworth, the headmaster was arrested, fined, and put under investigation, alongside the other headmasters of the orphanages that Elise had hit. They were charged with a seemingly endless list of wrongdoings, ranging from child abuse to fraud. The trials for the headmasters were set to begin in a week, starting with Mrs. Gallagher herself.

"Who do you think she is?" one of the boys asked the other on the bench.

"I don't know. She kind of looks like my older sister's friend. I think her name is Cheryl," his friend said, peering closer at the picture on the phone screen.

The other boy huffed. "Ravenkin's name isn't *Cheryl*. It's something cool and badass, just like her."

"Yeah, I guess you're right. She has to be really hot, though. I mean, look at her." He held up the phone so they could both see the image there.

The other boy nodded. "Probably."

Elise chuckled to herself as she passed by the pondering boys. Even after everything that happened at Havensworth, she had kept her identity a secret.

AFTER RUSHING INTO THE CROWD THAT DAY, SHE was surrounded by police officers, cameras, and random civilians just hoping to get a look at her. She tried to push her way through to her friends, but the sea of people constricted her in place. She remembered feeling suffocated, isolated. She called for people to move so she could get by, but no one listened.

Averin had squeezed her shoulder and held on for dear might as he ducked out of sight of the cameras and squawked at anyone who got too close to them. He was the only thing keeping anyone at bay. But even then, she couldn't see her escape.

"Ravenkin! What happened in there?"

"Ravenkin, where do you plan to hit next?"

"What are your plans for the future?"

"Can we expect to see you at the upcoming trials?"

"Ravenkin, show us your face!"

Elise shoved her way in between people, desperately trying to disappear, to be safe again. But then, she saw her friends in front of her. Orion reached out a hand, and when she squeezed it tight, he yanked her and Averin out of the crowd. She, Orion, Beth, and Averin fled the scene, running through the streets and down several alleyways until the crowd dissipated, and anyone following them lost their trail. Once they were in the clear, Elise slipped off her mask, gently slid Averin into the tote bag that Beth always carried with her, and they all made their way to the nearest veterinary clinic.

Elise had Averin's wing checked out, not without a few wary glances and odd looks at the group of kids bringing an injured raven into the clinic. But when the vet told them that Averin would be okay, and that he merely needed rest and to keep the wing crutched for a few days, Elise couldn't contain her relief.

The four of them practically skipped to the park that afternoon and met up with the rest of the Blackwings. They were also relieved by the good news and welcomed Averin back with gentle pats and *coos*. They all settled on their bench together and soaked in the relief, the sunshine, and the overwhelming sense of accomplishment. But something scratched at Elise's mind. She couldn't settle quite yet.

"I think Havensworth will be our last hit," she said. It wasn't easy to say, and it was even harder to swallow. But for the sake of her friends and their safety, she couldn't risk doing any more hits.

She expected a sigh of relief and an "I told you so" from Beth, but what she found when she looked up was an expression of exasperation.

"Are you kidding me?" her friend asked.

"No. We messed up, and the plan failed. Sure, it worked out in the end, but one of our own got hurt. I'm not risking that again."

"Elise, you can't just stop now."

"I thought that's what you wanted all along."

"Well, yeah, at first." Beth bit her lip. "But... look, you were right, okay? Every single hit we do has risks involved. We all agreed to it, and that's that. It sucks what happened and that Averin got hurt, but you can't just let that stop you."

Elise shook her head, her voice rising. "I can't see

any one of you get hurt again—human or raven. I can't. And if that means the hits end, then so be it."

Orion sighed gently. "Elise, no one blames you for what happened. It was an accident and a mistake. But we'll be better next time. We'll plan better so no one gets hurt."

"We can only plan so much! There are always going to be unknown variables, and I can't—" Elise balled her hands into tight fists as the echoes of Averin's pained screeches and her ravens' calls for help flittered in her mind. "I can't risk it."

Everyone grew quiet, none of them knowing how to move forward from here. But then Averin's even and commanding voice resounded in Elise's mind.

"It's not your fault, Elise."

Elise looked up at him. "It is. All of it is. And I can't risk doing it again, Averin."

Averin looked at her, long and pointed. He tilted his head as he always did.

"I accepted the risk. It isn't your fault. And I would like to keep going."

Elise's eyes widened. "Really? Even after everything?"

Averin nodded. "Really."

Elise looked over to the rest of the Blackwings, and they also nodded and bobbed their heads in agreement. They had wanted to continue on their path, no matter the risks. They wanted to continue to help kids feel safe again in the city.

And so, with the help of the Blackwings, Beth, and Orion, they resumed their fight. They continued with orphanages for a while, and then started to pick up homeless shelters, boarding homes, and even certain public schools. They found where the forgotten children of the city were, they discovered the abuse that plagued them, and they made a plan to eradicate the source of it.

And now, two months later and glowing in the warm sunlight of Spring, Elise walked up to her bench and handed Orion the vanilla cone in her other hand. She sat down beside him and nestled in close as he thanked her with a kiss before licking his own ice cream. She smiled as his milk mustache formed, but she didn't try to wipe it away.

She opened the bag of cone pieces, and at the sound of the Ziploc opening, she found the Blackwings eagerly awaiting their snack on the wall opposite her. She laughed as she threw them pieces of cones and watched as each of them hawk down the crunchy pieces, as they always did.

Averin was slow and deliberate, as usual. But finally, after many weeks, he could fly again. His wing was back to normal, and other than a slight twinge of pain here and there, he said it seemed completely healed. Elise worried, but Averin always assured her that it was healing just fine, and he, too, was just fine.

"They love their ice cream cones, don't they?" Orion chuckled before licking at his own again.

Elise nodded, her smile tender as she watched the Blackwings munch on their snacks. Averin looked up at her as if sensing her fond gaze. She couldn't stop her soft side from sneaking out.

"Thank you, Averin."

Averin tilted his head at her. "For what, exactly? You brought *us* the cone pieces."

Elise laughed, the sound easy on her throat and music to her ears. She hadn't laughed so much for... well, her entire life, really. But these last few months with her ravens, her friends, her family, and Orion— they had transformed her into something softer, kinder, and much more at peace.

"Not for the snacks. I mean... thank you. For everything. For keeping me company all those times in the park. For listening to me when I needed to vent. For standing up for me and protecting me when no one else would. You brought me into the Blackwings, and you made me one of your own. And that... I'll never be able to fully repay your kindness, but I'm going to try my best."

Elise grinned at her friend, who tilted his head in response. He clucked his approval just as all the others followed suit.

"Keep bringing us these cone pieces, and the debt will be repaid in no time!" Vrukum squawked.

The others chuckled and flapped at him for intruding on a such a serious moment, but Elise was relieved for the break in tension. She laughed as all her birds hopped down from the wall and jumped onto the bench between her and Orion, and on her lap. They nestled into her, and she laughed, loud and throaty, as she patted each of them on the head.

These ravens weren't just regular birds. They weren't dumb or evil or mischievous or unkind like all the stereotypes had made them out to be. They were smart, they were kind and loving, and they were loyal to their pack. She wouldn't trade them for the world.

"Thanks to you, not only has my own life improved, but we've improved the lives of every child we've saved in the city. None of this would have happened without you guys. So, from me to you, for every child in this city —*thank you*. All of you," Elise finished.

The birds cooed and cawed at her as they nudged her lovingly.

"We wouldn't have it any other way!" Kani screeched.

"You're one of us!" Kumi seconded her twin.

"Life's been a lot more fun with you around, Elise!" Vrukum clucked.

Dolvek nodded once.

And then Averin, sturdy, even, and watchful

Averin. Elise met his gaze with glistening eyes, experiencing tears caused by overwhelming happiness for the first time in her entire life. Averin nodded in agreement, his pearly eyes like two bright suns.

"The Blackwings are for life. And until the end, you will always have a place in our flock. Always, Elise."

Elise's eyes welled with tears, and she fought to keep them in. Orion and the birds chuckled and squawked at her soft side, but she waved them off as she wiped her face. She focused her attention on the rapidly melting ice cream cone in her hand instead and made headway on cleaning up the drips running down the sides.

She finished it just as a high-pitched voice yelled from the left. Elise looked up and found Lily, Thomas, and Beth heading in their direction.

Lily skipped down the sidewalk, singing the theme song to one of her favorite cartoons out loud as Thomas raced past her on the right. She jogged to keep up, but he crashed into the bench first.

"First! I win!" Thomas yelled.

Lily pouted. "You never said we were racing. That's not fair."

Thomas shrugged, but even he was winded after his long sprint. He sprawled on the sidewalk in front of them as he caught his breath, and Lily forgot all about the last-minute race as she turned to pull Elise into a tight squeeze.

"Elise! Sorry we're late. *Thomas* had to finish the last of his math homework." She groaned.

Thomas peeked an eye open from behind the cover of his arm. "Hey! Fractions are tougher than you think. Just you wait; you'll see when you're older."

"Whatever, we'll see about that." Lily pursed her lips before she caught sight of Orion's nearly finished ice cream. "Aw! You guys got ice cream already?"

Orion nodded sheepishly. "Sorry, Lil. We were getting hot here in the sun while we waited for you guys."

Lily pouted, and Beth, who had just managed to join them after taking her time walking to the group instead of sprinting, flicked her arm gently. "Quit pouting. We have plenty of ice cream at home."

"But it's not the same!" Lily whined.

Elise knew that Beth and Lily could each argue their points to the grave, so she stepped in before they delved too deep into this hold. She rubbed a hand over the top of Lily's head, ruffling her hair. "We'll get more later. Don't you worry."

"Really?"

"Of course." Elise smiled. "Whatever you want."

Lily squealed with uncontained glee, and even Thomas pumped his fist into the air in excitement. Beth gave Elise a look, but she shrugged. It was warm outside, they had no plans, and they were free to do as they pleased. They were happy, they were safe, and things were... perfect. She didn't want to ruin this picture-perfect day with senseless bickering.

"Hey, look!" Thomas pointed up at the trees, where the Blackwings had flocked to when the younger kids sprinted toward the bench. "There are ravens up there. Do you think they helped Ravenkin bring down the headmasters of those orphanages?"

Lily peered up at them, too. "Maybe. They're so big! No wonder all the bad people are so scared of them."

Thomas chuckled. "Yeah. They're so cool."

"Yeah," Lily agreed, her little voice fading out as she looked at the birds in wonder.

Beth gave Elise a knowing look, and Orion squeezed her hand lightly. Elise smiled at her friends, both human and bird. Even though the young ones didn't know her secret yet, she was certain that she would tell them one day.

One day, when they were older, when they might understand the responsibility that laid on her shoulders. But for now, she basked in the contentment she felt with her entire family nestled together on her bench in the corner of the park. This was where her new life had begun, not only as Ravenkin, but as Elise Winters—happy and free.

As they all laughed and joked that afternoon, basking under the warm rays of sunshine that shone between the branches of the trees, and munching on ice cream cones that dripped down their fingers, Elise was more at ease, more content, and happier than she had ever been before.

She'd wanted a family to pick her, adopt her, and bring her to their home all her life. She wanted to be *wanted*. But now, surrounded by her friends and the Blackwings, she realized that her family had been around her all along.

This was her life now. This was her future. This was her family—and she wouldn't trade that for the world.

EPILOGUE

ELISE PACKED THE LAST OF HER THINGS INTO A small box in her shared bedroom.

Today was the day. After eighteen years in the system that she had fought so hard to better every day, she was finally leaving it.

Yesterday was her eighteenth birthday, and the kids, adults, and Ms. Augustine held the biggest party to celebrate it. She hadn't expected the party, as she usually celebrated her birthdays on her own or not at all because Mrs. Gallagher had always forbidden celebrations, and Elise didn't have anyone to celebrate with, really. But those two things had changed in the last six months. She had a family now to celebrate with. And Mrs. Gallagher—

Mrs. Gallagher finally had her trial, and what they all expected to drag on for days—maybe weeks—lasted only two days. And then the verdict gave them all the more reason to celebrate—Mrs. Gallagher was fined half a million dollars and sent to prison for three years to serve her sentence. At hearing the news, the kids in the orphanage threw their own party, full of smiles and wild cheers.

Once the "Mrs. Gallagher Sentencing" party came to an end, the next event to look forward to was Elise's birthday.

Elise stressed for more reasons than one about turning eighteen. It meant she had to leave the orphanage, find a place to stay, *pay* for a place to stay, and get a job to support herself on her own. She barely graduated high school before her eighteenth birthday hit, so she felt like she couldn't even fully celebrate it.

But Ms. Augustine and her friends, as supportive and caring as ever, helped her every step of the way. Ms. Augustine even reached out to a local college, one

that she had personal connections to, that, coinciden-
tally, had a specific program that was tailored toward
orphaned children or children leaving the system. It
offered reduced payments, more scholarships to cover
the costs of school, and it offered housing for those
students at a discounted rate.

Elise had never thought of going to college before.
How could she? Mrs. Gallagher never let her succeed
in school, and between her teachers and the classmates
who sabotaged her, she had no support at school.

She always enjoyed learning, and she wanted to
attend a college after high school, but that always
seemed like a far-off dream. But with the help of Ms.
Augustine pulling some favors and digging deep into
her network, Elise got an interview with the dean the
very next day.

She remembered being covered in a layer of
sweat, and painstakingly trying to ignore it after she
had spent hours picking out the right clothes with
Ms. Augustine for the interview. When she stepped
inside the dean's office, she didn't know what to
expect. But the man was gentle, and his deep smile
lines showed that he wasn't pretending to be happy to
see her.

She spent nearly two hours talking to the dean that
day. She told him her life story, or a shortened version
of it, what had changed over the most recent months,
and of her passion in continuing her education. No
matter her background, she wanted to persevere and do

what she could to give herself a bright, wide-open future.

"What do you see yourself majoring in?" the dean had asked.

She didn't even hesitate. "Social work."

"Really. After everything you've been through?"

Elise nodded easily. "I want to make the lives of lost and forgotten children as happy and as fruitful as I can. They're already alone or struggling in this world. I want to give them the chance to succeed and know that they, too, are loved and supported."

The dean had given her a long look, but for the first time that day, Elise wasn't nervous. He chuckled and held out his hand for her to shake.

"It's been excellent meeting with you today, Elise. I know you'll be a fine addition to our institution."

Elise could barely contain her joy as she violently shook the man's hand and thanked him ten-fold for meeting with and listening to her. She ran back to the orphanage that day and grinned wide and bright as she told everyone the news.

She got in!

OVER THE COMING WEEKS, SHE WORKED WITH THE registrar's office to sign up for classes, with housing to set up her dorm room living arrangement on campus, and with the financial aid department, who explained to her the costs, which were minimal at worst. She could cover those with her new job at the local bookstore!

It was happening. Elise was going to go to college. She was going to get an education. She wasn't going to be in mounds and mounds of debt. And she'd have a place to stay for the next four years while she earned her degree.

She could barely wait to turn eighteen after that. And Ms. Augustine and the kids at the orphanage didn't disappoint. They threw a huge surprise party the day of and shocked her with their wild cheers and congratulations as she stepped through the door after work one afternoon.

"Happy birthday, Elise!"

There were decorations covering every surface inside the main living area, there were tables filled to the brim with her favorite snacks and meals, there was a pile of presents from the kids in the corner, and they played all of her favorite songs as they laughed and danced and played games together late into the evening.

Beth, Lily, and Thomas gave her their own gifts later when they all huddled in their shared bedroom as the activity outside died down.

Lily made a card for her, which they all signed with their names and messages wishing her the best after she left. They proclaimed their happiness for her and excitement for her future, even if they were sad to see her go. Elise sniffled as she set down the card, but she promised to visit. They were her family, after all.

Thomas gave her a copy of her favorite book, one she had read herself many times, but she had also read to it him and Lily when they wanted a bedtime story to help fall asleep. She accepted his gift with a beam.

Beth was last to hold out her small baggie, filled with purple tissue paper. Elise smiled at the choice of color, Beth knew it was her favorite. She pulled the tissue paper out and felt something cool like metal under her fingertips. She pulled it out and found an enamel pin in the shape of a raven, with both its wings out and its head turned to show its profile. It was powerful, it was dark, and it made her eyes burn with unshed tears. She pulled Beth into a tight hug and whispered into her hair.

"Thank you. For everything."

Beth squeezed her tight. "Thank you, Elise. We'll miss you all more than you know."

Elise held her friend for moments longer, and when both of them pulled away, they looked at each other with red-rimmed eyes and sniffling noses. They laughed, wiping each other's tears away before Lily and Thomas joined in on a group hug.

Elise gave her, now empty, shared room a once-over. Lily's pink bed sheets were rumpled and a bit short for her bed, but she refused to give them up because she loved the pattern on her blankets. Thomas' bed was messy and unmade, as usual. But he kept his first stuffed animal—a ratty bear he called Milo—tucked beside his pillow and just under his blankets. He couldn't bear to part with the creature, but he also wouldn't be caught dead carrying it around. Beth's bed was neatly made and lined with entirely too many pillows. But Elise paused to straighten them with a sad smile lining her lips.

Elise took a deep breath and grabbed her final box before she stepped out into the hall and pulled the door to her room shut. In a way, it felt like a rite of passage. After eighteen years spent in a shared bedroom, she was going to be moving into a dorm room with one other roommate. It wouldn't be totally differ-ent, she figured. But that roommate wasn't her best friend, and they weren't her family that she lived with, cried with, and laughed with every day.

Elise choked down the lump in her throat as she walked down the steps to the main living room. All of the others waited there for her, Ms. Augustine, Beth, Lily, Thomas, and the rest of the kids at the orphanage. Even they looked on with sad smiles and sniffling noses.

She had gotten to know them all so well over the years, and truthfully, it sent a spear through her heart to know that she wouldn't see them every day, and she wouldn't be right by their sides at a moment's notice. But these kids were safe now and happier under the care of Ms. Augustine. They had futures; they had worry-free days ahead. With that in mind, Elise felt ready to move forward in her own life.

She hugged everyone goodbye and wished them all well. Ms. Augustine gave her yet another stack of papers to take with her, with directions to the college campus, how to get to her dorm, check-in times, and emergency contacts to reach out to with any issues. Elise laughed as she pulled her into a tight hug. Ms. Augustine wavered at first, but without another moment to spare, she squeezed Elise tight.

"Good luck, Elise. I know you'll do great things."

Elise sniffled, taking in one more whiff of the woman's sweet perfume she had come to remember and love so much. "Thank you... for everything. I'll be back to visit soon enough. And you better visit me, okay?" Elise pulled back with a twisted grin.

Ms. Augustine wiped at her own eyes and nodded. "Of course. We'll all pay a visit when you've settled in."

"Good. I wouldn't have it any other way."

Elise turned to her friends then and held out her arms. Lily, Thomas, and Beth jumped forward and squeezed her tightly into a bear hug. They were the hardest goodbyes, and she knew very well that it wouldn't be easy to let go. But after their little gift exchange and moment in the bedroom a few nights before, she felt more certain than ever that they would be just fine without her.

"I love you guys," Elise whispered around the tight squeeze that Lily had her in.

Lily, Thomas, and Beth sniffled and squeezed her even tighter. "We love you, too," they chorused.

After a handful of more goodbyes and tight hugs, Elise stepped toward the door. She waved a hand at all of her friends and family, and promised to visit them again soon. With their final cries of "bye!" and "good luck!" and "visit soon," she stepped outside into the warm, sticky heat of the summer.

Orion waited in his car on the street out front. After passing his driver's test months before and earning his full license, he was eager to drive her around whenever she needed. A car meant freedom for him, so he was quick to buy something for himself once he was able to. His car was old and used, but it drove well and was reliable. That's all he asked for.

He organized the last of her boxes in the back and smiled when she came down the steps with one final box in her hands.

"Ready?" he asked, reaching for the last box.

Elise handed it to him, and he set it in a cranny between two other boxes, filling the back of the car to capacity. He closed the trunk and gave her a wink, and she couldn't stop her face from turning red.

"Ready."

Orion hopped into the driver's side, and Elise into the passenger's seat, and after buckling up, Orion pulled away from the curb. Elise looked over her shoulder at the orphanage that had been her shelter for so long, and over the last few months, she finally felt able to call her home.

She wiped at her eyes as she imagined her friends inside, teary-eyed and shuffling back to their room. The room that she had shared with them. The room that housed their planning meetings for future hits with the Blackwings. The room that she would not return to that evening.

Elise turned back around in her seat and blew her nose with a tissue that she grabbed from the box on the floor.

"Are you excited?" Orion asked.

She nodded slowly. "Why is leaving behind what you have so painful? Am I doing the right thing?"

Orion gave her a quick glance before looking back toward the road. "Elise—of course. It's painful because that's your family, that's your life, and it has been for years. But it's time to move forward. Besides, your family won't be far away, right?"

Elise swallowed past the lump in her throat. "Yeah, I guess not."

"Hey," Orion took her hand in his and squeezed it gently. "You have us, all of us, supporting you. We're not far, you know that. But it's your time now. Time to focus on you and your future, because you, Elise Winters, are going to do amazing things."

Elise glanced at him. "You think so?"

Orion smiled. "I know so."

Elise gave his hand a gentle squeeze, and she didn't let go the whole way as he drove her to the school. He pulled up outside her dorm and turned the car off. They glanced around at the many kids carrying bags and boxes alongside their parents and siblings into the dorms. Elise felt like the odd one to only have four boxes total for herself.

"Well, this is it." Orion clicked his seatbelt off.

Elise took a deep, steadying breath, trying to calm the heart racing in her chest. Something black fluttered in her peripheral, and she looked out her window. There, she saw them—the Blackwings lingered in the trees outside her dorm. They watched her with eager, bright eyes. Elise smiled at them, nodding once at Averin, whose pearly gaze bobbed as he nodded in return.

This was it. This was her future. And she was ready to dive in head first.

Elise clicked open her door and stepped outside into the summer heat as the other students moved around her. She popped open the trunk of the car and grabbed her first box.

She was ready.

RAVENKIN

VIOLA TEMPEST